SATANIC SEDUCTIONS

Demonic Gay Sex Stories

PETER SCHUTES
ADAM MAXWELL BIGGLESWORTH

Three stories, one message: Demons are not to be trusted.

DECEIVED BY THE DEMON - AKA DECEIVED, CURSED, AND BLESSED

This cautionary tale was initially entitled The Monkey's Pudendum. Using the same irony as its namesake, "The Monkey's Paw," a mysterious stranger promises Rowan Mallory his deepest desire: his little curse will expand, and he will be "the biggest in town." The stranger grants Rowan's wish in its most literal sense. This painful condition comes with an additional demonic curse that prevents him from forming lasting connections. The hero leaves his small town for adventures in big cities. Lonely and burdened with a monster between his legs, Max works to undo his curse. Can he be free of his enormous burden?

SATAN'S SISSY BOY

This demonic sissy transformation short story is another ironic tale of deception in the same tradition as O. Henry's Gift of the Magi or The Monkey's Paw. When Paul Harris has no luck with women, he never realizes it's because of his tiny endowment. When he meets a stranger who promises him a close relationship with a woman, he accepts the curse with hellish consequences.

CLOISTERED

Vicente knows three things:

1 He's too well-endowed to ever be with a woman and thus destined to be a gay Priest.

2 His luxurious accommodations at the Vatican are a gilded cage that enslaves him to a demonic cult.

3 He has finally found love with a fellow priest, but they are doomed if he cannot break free of his bondage.

How will he free himself of his sexual slavery?

CONTENTS

BOOK ONE – DECEIVED BY THE DEMON

1. Barbax Woods — 3
2. Not Gone But Forgotten — 9
3. Max Is Born — 12
4. The Ticket Master — 16
5. The Windy City Tailor — 22
6. Young Man's Christian Association — 27
7. The Oldest Profession — 31
8. Tailored For Maximum Effect — 35
9. The Accountant — 39
10. Flight From Winter — 42
11. Flight Attendant From Hell — 45
12. The City of Angels — 48
13. Too Big for His Britches — 51
14. The Strip — 54
15. Dante's Hole — 57
16. Honor Among Thieves — 60
17. The Country Club — 62
18. Santa Monica — 64
19. Searching — 68
20. Long John — 71
21. Tip Your Waiter — 76
22. A Friendship Like No Other — 78
23. Marmont Revisited — 81
24. Friends to Lovers — 85
25. Terrible Bedside Manner — 90
26. Palmistry — 92
27. Door to Door Salesman — 95
28. Rumpelstiltskin — 97
Epilogue — 102

BOOK TWO – DEMONIZED: STRAIGHT TO SISSY

Satan's Little Sissy   107

BOOK THREE – CLOISTERED: FUCKING WITH THE DEMON

1. One Man's Blessing   121
2. The Guadalajara Branch   124
3. French Kiss   129
4. Cabin Fever   135
5. The Pope's House   141
6. The Gilded Cage   150
7. Paying the Piper   157
8. Hatching a Plan   168
9. The Way Out   172
10. Benedictine Bliss   177
About Peter Schutes   181
About Adam Maxwell Bigglesworth   183
Other Books from Peter Schutes Publishing   185

BOOK ONE – DECEIVED BY THE DEMON

AKA: Deceived, Cursed, and Blessed

by Peter Schutes

BARBAX WOODS

In Defiance, Ohio, in the year 1930, Rowan Mallory was a strong, attractive young man. Dark brown hair framed his symmetrical face. His nose was slightly crooked, making him all the more handsome. As in many things in life, a flaw can bring out the beauty.

Rowan had a flaw of which he was deeply ashamed. When all the other boys in junior high got their growth spurt, Rowan did, too, except in one place. Even when he reached full maturity, his penis remained as tiny as a toddler's. He constantly compared himself to the other guys in the locker room while doing his best to hide his shameful secret. His sadness grew with every penis he glimpsed. His was truly the smallest in school. He dropped out of football because he couldn't stand the showers. The other players jeered and called him "Princess Tinymeat." Soon everyone in high school, male or female, knew that Rowan Mallory carried the curse. His dating prospects dried up. The girls giggled when he walked past.

A few of his male classmates reached out and tried to comfort him, but he spiraled into a depression that never lifted. He was too depressed to apply for college. When he graduated, Howie Ward, one of his former teammates, patted him on the back. Rowan didn't realize that it was a prank. Taped to the back of his graduation gown was a crudely drawn sign that read, "I have a teeny weeny peeny." He didn't discover it until the ceremony was over. He put Howie on a list of revenge fantasies.

❧

A STRANGE THING HAPPENED TO ROWAN AFTER graduation. His sexual fantasies grew out of his obsession with size. He imagined having a gargantuan cock. The weird part was how he dreamed of using it. He wanted to fuck Howie and all those mean jocks in the ass. He would make them plead for mercy as he tore into their bowels. He pushed the thoughts out of his mind, but they only returned more intensely. He wanted to fuck every man's ass and make them pay for humiliating him so publicly.

The obsession grew to encompass all men. The men with large buttocks appealed to him most. If he saw a voluptuous male ass, his tiny penis grew hard, not that anyone could tell. He spent hours washing his hands in public restrooms to glimpse a big one. He discovered that men with normal-sized penises (or big ones) often fucked each other in the stalls. He had no desire to get fucked. He wanted to do all the fucking, but he didn't have the proper equipment.

His job that summer was in a bottling plant. Prohibition had ended, and liquor production created a vast job market in an otherwise depressed economy. He still lived at home. His walk to the factory took about an hour. If he were willing to cut through the Barbax Woods, it would cut the walk to fifteen minutes. Nobody went through those woods. Old stories dating to the town's settlement warned of evil lurking in the trees. Children had gone missing, and several grown men were committed to a sanatorium after daring to cross.

Rowan's size obsession was eating a hole in his soul. Each morning when he awoke, he felt he couldn't face another day with his small penis. One day, washing his hands in the restroom at the factory, Jeff Gross walked in. He planted himself before the urinal, stepped back, and unraveled a fire hose penis from his dungarees. It was twenty or thirty times the size of Rowan's tiny nub, which hardened like a nipple at the sight of it.

Jeff saw Rowan staring unabashedly.

"You want to hold it?" He grinned. "It's not all that great. I can't get laid to save my life."

Rowan remained speechless.

"Nobody, man. Not women. Not even men." Jeff paused to gauge Rowan's reaction. He didn't get a clear reading, so he continued. "You got a pretty sweet ass and no dick to get in the way. Why don't you let me fuck you in that stall right there?"

Finally, Rowan spoke. "I'm not a disgusting faggot like you."

Jeff shrugged. He had that horrible confidence only a well-hung man can possess. "It's your loss. When your dick is this big, you gotta catch as catch can." He folded his dick twice before stuffing it into his underwear.

☙❧

ROWAN OBSESSED OVER JEFF AND HIS MONSTER PENIS. The hole in his soul was tearing apart further. He barely ate his supper and turned in early, crying himself to sleep.

He awoke at 8:30. He had to be at work in thirty minutes! His dad had already left in the truck, and his mom didn't know how to drive.

He threw on his clothes and ran down the block. He couldn't run long distances and knew he would be late.

As anyone who has lived with depression knows, being late to work is a frequent problem. Rowan had two warnings; a third would get him fired.

Casting all superstitions aside, Rowan left the sidewalk and entered Barbax Woods. Unlike other forests, Barbax was completely silent. No wind rustled through the deciduous leaves. No birds called. The hush was deafening.

Rowan felt a goose walk over his grave. The hairs on his arms stood up. Maybe the old legends were true. He didn't care. After seeing Jeff Gross and his colossal penis, Rowan didn't care if he lived or died. His life was so miserable; how could death be any worse?

"Life is precious." A voice startled him. He whirled to see who said it. Nobody was there.

"Who said that?"

He scanned the trees and saw a clearing just ahead. As he drew closer, he saw a startlingly handsome man with black curly hair, green eyes, and a well-trimmed beard. He sat on a stump.

"I did," said the handsome man.

Jeff was drawn to this handsome stranger like a bee to a bright flower. The man smiled.

"Come, son, don't be afraid."

Rowan felt an intense power radiating off this man. 'What are you doing here?"

"I could ask you the same, Rowan. These are my woods. Why are you here?"

"I'm late for work."

The curly-haired stranger nodded. "I know why you're really here. You don't even know yet."

Rowan frowned. "If you're going to kill me, just get it over with. I'm done with the world anyway."

The handsome stranger laughed. "I've seen your future, and you won't be leaving any time soon."

Rowan glanced at his watch. "I'm going to be late, so can I go?"

The stranger smiled. "Don't you want to know how I know your name and future? How I know about that tiny penis that torments you?"

Rowan said, "You don't know me. Everyone in town probably knows about my miserable little dick. And I'm late. I can't lose my job."

The stranger pointed at Rowan's watch. "Take a closer look. Time has no sway over this place."

Rowan saw that his watch had stopped. Who was this guy?

As if he could hear his thoughts, the handsome man said, "You know who I am. I go by many names. I'm the angel who answers the calls of the brokenhearted. I repair those hearts in exchange for very little. I am Barbax."

Rowan still thought this man was a charlatan. "Prove it."

"Make a wish."

"I wish I had the biggest dick in town."

Barbax smiled. "I know. And I am prepared to give it to you as long as you are willing to bargain for it."

Rowan shrugged. "Go on. What do you want from me?"

"Your soul, of course. But also, I need to keep the balance, so we need to include some clauses."

Rowan shrugged again. "It's all make-believe, so whatever you want."

Now the stranger frowned. "This isn't binding if you think it's make-believe. I'll tell you what. I'm going to give you a free sample. No obligation. Two free inches."

Barbax snapped his fingers.

Rowan gasped. The mostly empty space between his legs was not so empty.

"Go ahead, Rowan, check it out."

Rowan unbuttoned his trousers and looked down at his penis, which was still very small, but not miserably so. "Holy shit!"

The handsome stranger nodded. "It's some shit, but it ain't holy."

Rowan felt a cloud of misery lift instantly. It was as if the entire nineteen years had been a bad dream. He was almost within the "normal" range now. But the hunger for size was insatiable. He was determined to make this bargain with Barbax.

"I'm glad you're convinced, Rowan. Your soul is already mending quickly; it's no use to me in its current state, but I'm willing to bet you will give me a whole soul when the time finally comes."

Rowan barely heard the man. His mind was racing with the chance to realize a truly impossible dream. He was going to fuck every one of those football players in the ass and make them scream for more. "Yeah, you need a whole soul."

"I can tell your mind is made up, so let's bargain. I will give you a few extra powers along with your main wish. Those are the clauses. You'll see how they work once this bargain is struck. You simply need to state your wish out loud."

"Can't you tell me now?"

The stranger laughed. "This is a bargain, not a negotiation."

Rowan hadn't.

"No matter. Please state your wish out loud. And think very, very carefully before you make it. The results are permanent and binding.

Rowan paused to consider his words, then said, "I want the biggest, longest, thickest dick in town."

"Done."

❧ 2 ❧

NOT GONE BUT
FORGOTTEN

The man vanished in a puff of smoke. Rowan checked his watch. The second hand had begun to sweep. He felt the flesh between his legs expand and lengthen with each step. By the time he reached work, his underwear strained to contain the growing mass.

Rowan clocked in exactly on time. He ran to the restroom and locked himself in the stall. He could barely get the log of cock out of his pants. It was bigger than Jeff's, and it was the kind that got longer and thicker when it got hard. He watched it double in volume as it filled with blood. Hard, it was obscene.

Masturbation was a tedious necessity in the past. Rowan typically used a thumb and forefinger to bring himself to orgasm. Now his cock was so huge that he wasn't sure two hands would do the trick. He was so aroused now; his cock would never go down until he shot his load. He pointed his cock towards the toilet and jerked it with two hands. The feeling of having so much flesh in his hands was intoxicating. He feared he might never leave this restroom if he didn't cum. There was no way to get it into his pants in its current state. Luckily, after five minutes of hard jacking, his new colossal cock cooperated. When he came, he nearly fainted. The toilet filled with buckets of thick hot cum.

A voice came from the next stall. "Damn!" There was a little peephole, and someone had been watching him. Pride and embarrassment fought for dominance in Rowan's mind. Pride won.

"You like it?"

"I love it. Can I touch it?"

Rowan knelt on the floor and let his long cock slide under the stall wall. The man in the next stall picked it up lovingly and stroked it. He licked the remaining cum from the head.

Rowan tested the waters. "You want me to fuck you?"

The man laughed. "Have you ever fucked anyone with that? Are they still alive?"

Rowan felt the strangest sensation of shame over his new size. It wasn't as devastating as the old one, but it was a shame of another color. He shook his head and focused.

"Suck it, then."

The man tried his best but could only get a third of the head into his mouth. It was too thick. He licked the pee hole and the surrounding flesh, but it was no use.

A third man entered the restroom, ending the possibility of any under-stall fun. Rowan was used to pulling up his underwear without resistance. This new cock required considerable unpacking, unlike anything he was used to. He pictured Jeff Gross folding his dick twice. He tried it, but it was so thick that it made a ridiculous bulge. He was going to have to wear it down one leg. After several minutes of fumbling, he was able to zip up. His left leg looked swollen compared to his right, but it was the best he could do.

He took his place on the assembly line just before the equipment started up. His manager approached him. "Can I help you, sir?"

Rowan frowned. "Hey, Mr. Klein, what's up?"

His boss said, "I don't believe we've met, son."

Rowan slapped gummed labels on bottles as they rolled past. "Mr. K, it's me, Rowan Mallory."

Klein snorted. "I don't know who you are, but I'm a man short, so you can keep at it, for now."

Rowan saw Jeff Gross and smiled. Jeff looked at him blankly. Rowan was a stranger. As the realization washed over him, he broke into a sweat. People whispered and pointed. A few eyes strayed below his belt. He always dreamed of being looked at this way, but the failure to be recognized by anyone in the plant overshadowed any sense of joy.

Rowan ran to the restroom to look in the mirror. It was still the same face looking back. He hadn't changed. People had simply forgotten him.

3

MAX IS BORN

When Rowan told the supervisor he was sick, he gave no reaction other than a shrug. He ran out of the factory and into the woods.

"Hello?" He shouted. The eerie hush was his only response. He found his way to the clearing.

"What have you done to me? God Damn you!"

"He already did, ages ago." The demon Barbax sat on a stump, staring at his latest creation.

Rowan said, "Nobody knew who I was."

The demon smiled. "That was one of the clauses. You were tired of being Princess Tinymeat. This gives you a clean slate. Basically, you are erased. There may be some lingering effects for a while. People may forget you right after meeting you. It's unpredictable, really. But you are not Rowan Mallory. At least, not the Rowan Mallory that lives here in this two-horse town. You are whoever you want to be."

"Surely my parents will remember me?"

The devil shook his head. "I wouldn't bother going back there. They'll probably call the cops because a stranger broke into their home."

"You didn't tell me this was part of the bargain!"

"That's why it's a bargain, not a negotiation. It's a grab bag. You got the biggest dick in town. So what if people don't remember the old you? You don't care. You are no longer Rowan Mallory. Pick a new identity."

As the words left the demon's lips, they had a hypnotic effect. Rowan suddenly didn't give a damn about the Rowan he had been. He was somebody new. He picked the first name that popped into his head.

"Max Andrews."

The demon smiled and nodded. "You're getting it. Reinvent yourself. Over and over everywhere you go."

Rowan saw Barbax in a new light. He was freeing him from the bondage of his old self. He loved his mother and father, but they don't remember him. They're probably up in his old bedroom, saying, "Now, where on earth did all this stuff come from?" He would have shed a tear, but he was numb now. He had lost all emotion. He felt primal urges - hunger, lust, fear, self-preservation. But love, caring, sadness, remorse - every higher emotion had left him. He was a different person. Almost a different species.

The dark stranger interrupted his thoughts. "I created something new. Now I want to test the merchandise." He unbuttoned his shirt, revealing a masculine, hairy chest. Muscles rippled as he pulled the shirt off. When he dropped his trousers and knelt on the old tree stump, exposing a loose anus that looked like a volcano. Rowan - now Max - needed no further prompting. He stepped forward and let his pants fall. Max's colossal chunk of meat swelled and stretched until it was fully hard and pointed at the demon's ass.

Slowly, he inserted his glans up to the corona. It was only then that he felt any resistance. The handsome hellhound was impatient.

"Fuck me."

With a loud pop, the corona pushed past the entryway, and then the long, heavy log of flesh entered the gaping hole, making a slurping sound. Max marveled at how easily his gargantuan cock slipped inside the handsome stranger. After an eternity, Max pressed his hips against the demon's buttocks. He wasn't an anatomy expert, but the whole process had been too easy. He should have hit something along the way.

"I'm built to accommodate anything." The demon could hear his thoughts. "Now revenge fuck me like I'm Howie Ward."

Max felt powerful male hormones surge as he began masterfully fucking the dark spirit. His thighs slapped against the big, round ass. Max caressed it and felt even more aroused. He couldn't believe he was so fucking massive. He took long strokes like the coupling rod on a locomotive. Barbax moaned.

"Oh, right there, Max. Right there. Just like that! Oh!"

Max had never known this kind of satisfaction. Compared to his thumb and forefinger, the demon's guts felt sublime. His whole huge long thick cock was surrounded entirely by angelic flesh. He could almost swear that the endless asshole was stroking him with peristaltic spasms. Even though he had just blown his load in the restroom an hour earlier, he was close to climax again. Barbax said, "You gotta cum inside me. All the way inside me. Oh, Christ! You're so big. I wanted you to have the best cock a soul could buy. You got the best cock. You got the best cock!" The devil unleashed a torrent of cum onto the old stump. He hadn't even touched himself.

"I'm cumming." Max closed his eyes. He was a virgin. Losing his virginity to the demon was surreal.

In spurts and gushes, the semen left Max and flooded the loose anus of the Devil. Some of it sprayed backward onto Max. He finished with a hard final thrust.

The Devil stood and walked a few steps forward, letting Max's knee-length cock and a river of semen exit the swollen hole.

"Was I any good?" Max was anxious.

"If you have to ask, it means you can do better."

"Really?"

"It was fucking great. Better than most. Definitely, the best virgin I've ever had. You reminded me that God doesn't know what a reward it was to bind me to Earth. Heaven is for tight twats and featherweight cocks."

"Can't he hear you now?"

Barbax laughed. "He is asleep at the wheel, my friend. Look at the wars, the suffering. They're all his fault because he's too lazy to do anything about humans. At least I'm down here among you, offering you a way out."

"I never thought about it like that."

"Speaking of which, there's a small-breasted woman I need to go visit. Once she agrees to the bargain, I'm going to titty fuck her til I break her jaw."

"I need to know what else is hidden inside the bargain, Barbax."

The demon smiled. "I just taught you how to fuck. So that's out of the way. I gave you a lack of empathy, so seducing men will be easy. What else? Hmmmm. You'll have some surprises along the way. You'll know where to find me if you need further guidance."

And the imp vanished.

❧ 4 ❧

THE TICKET MASTER

The man formerly known as Rowan Mallory, currently Max Andrews, had an entire oyster of a world before him. Where to go? What to do next? He had a few dollars in his pocket. What could he do? He walked into town. A T&F bus to Chicago was due to arrive in three hours. The ticket was just under four dollars. The ticket master was none other than Howie Ward, the asshole who put the cruel sign on Rowan's back.

"Where to?"

Max said, "Howie?"

Howie frowned. "Do I know you?"

"No, I was reading the name tag."

Howie was a muscular jock who didn't get his football scholarship. To see him selling tickets at the T & F was reward enough. But Rowan, or Max, wanted more. He saw the whole seduction at once, like reading a game of chess in one of those books. He knew every move he was going to make. Some were unethical, but none of it was violent or deeply immoral. He saw the pathway to consensual sex with this knucklehead.

"Actually," Max said, "there's another reason I said your name. I'm a talent scout for Northwestern. I wish

I hadn't gotten sick and missed your game. I'd heard great things about you."

Howie blushed. Because he was tow-headed, his pink face looked almost red. "You were gonna come?"

Max nodded. "Why don't you show me some of your moves now?"

Howie smiled. "Meet me out back."

Max played quarterback, and Howie showed off his skills as a left guard, blocking imaginary players with his squat, muscular frame. His trousers were too tight for football, and as Max predicted, they tore at the crack of Howie's curvaceous ass. Howie wasn't wearing underwear, and as he bent or stretched, Max caught glimpses of the puckered butthole lined with downy blond hairs. He found it hard to fight off an erection.

"I've seen enough, Mr. Ward. We need to get you a scholarship, young man." He felt guilty saying it, but he knew that Howie wouldn't remember him after all this seduction was over.

"You mean it?"

Max nodded. "Do you have any safety pins in your office?"

"Why?"

Max put his finger through the hole in Howie's pants, grazing his anus. "We gotta close up your hole." He felt the puckered anus relax for a second.

Howie was magenta now. He brought Max into the back office through a side door. He was the only employee in this small-town bus depot. He did janitorial and clerical work and mainly sold tickets. Howie handed a couple of safety pins to Max. "How do we do this?"

Max said, "It'd be easier if you took off your pants."

"I ain't got no underwear, man."

"If it helps any, I'll take my pants off, too. Would that make you comfortable?"

Howie chuckled. "Yeah, probably. Don't try no funny stuff."

Together they took off their pants. Howie was hung average, maybe even a little on the small side. When the ticket master caught a glimpse of the monster between Max's legs, he sucked in air hard and whistled. "Shit! That's a huge fucking dick."

Max stepped closer. "I can tell you want to hold it. It's okay. Everyone does."

Howie didn't waste a second. He grabbed the enormous cock with both hands and weighed it.

"Dude, do you ever get laid?"

Max smiled. "It's too big for women. I only ever find men who aren't too chickenshit to try it. Most don't make it. They have to be jocks, you know, familiar with pain, willing to take one for the team."

Howie stroked Max unconsciously. Max got a raging hard-on in seconds. Howie nearly screamed as the soft monster became a brutal giant. "Holy shit! You could put an eye out doing that!"

Max chuckled. "It's too bad you're not into funny stuff. I'd bet you're the type of jock that can handle pain. I'd fuck you so fast."

Howie drew his own conclusion. He wanted that scholarship I had offered. He wanted to make me happy.

"I ain't afraid of a little pain. I think that's gonna hurt really bad, though."

It was the tense of the verb he used. He said "gonna" not "would". It was just as he had predicted. Now he was three moves away from checkmate.

"It won't hurt once you relax."

"It won't?"

"I promise. You'll feel pain at first, but it will turn to pleasure in no time."

"Dude, let's do this!"

Howie grabbed a suspicious tub of Vaseline from his

desk drawer and smeared Max's cock before bending over. He rested his arms on the desktop and put his head to one side like a primary school student taking a seated nap.

Max took three minutes with his tongue, loosening up the tight jock hole and filling it with slippery spit. He stood and positioned the giant glans at the mouth of the anus.

"Don't worry. If it hurts, you'll just forget all about it."

Howie wiggled with dread and anticipation. Max pushed in an inch of his cock head before Howie reached back and pushed his thigh. "Slowly."

Max could go fast or slow, and Howie wouldn't remember anyway. He had been pretty fast with Barbax. He supposed he could take it slow for Howie, no matter how much he hated him. None of that old hate mattered now, anyway. He had the biggest dick in town. The sign Howie slapped on his back at graduation was wrong, mistaken. Howie slapped that sign on Rowan's back, not Max's.

Howie withdrew his hand and nodded. Max pushed further, but it was getting to the corona, and Howie's anus was stretched abnormally wide. Then, with a loud pop, the head found its way into the ticket agent's rectum.

"Oh, jeez! Oh, man. Ow!" Howie's hand pushed Max's thigh again. But Max knew he had to keep going to make it hurt less. He pushed in two more inches and paused. His cock was about a third of the way in.

"It fucking hurts!" Howie's tears didn't evoke sympathy.

"Just wait a bit. It'll feel good, I promise. Push out like you're trying to take a poop."

Howie obeyed. Max felt the waves of peristalsis pushing against him, but he also felt the inner anus loosen. He pushed another three inches into the boy.

Nearly halfway in. Just seven inches to go. That's when he felt the rectum come to an end. He couldn't go any deeper, but he tried. It made Howie piss himself.

"No more!"

But Max felt an instinctive urge to move to the left and push again. Now his cock forced itself deeper, entering the sigmoid colon. Howie's eyes fluttered.

"Oh shit, that's good. Dude, fuck me!"

Max didn't need further encouragement. He took long, deep strokes, sliding past the rectum and deep into the colon.

Max grunted. "Fuck you got a tight ass!"

Howie moaned. His head hung, and tears left his eyes. They were tears of ecstatic joy.

"Make me your bitch."

Max obliged. He found his rhythm and proceeded to tunnel deep inside his tormentor. Back and forth, with nothing blocking his way, he felt like he was fucking the Devil again. He had carved a passageway in Howie that let him all the way in. He found that if he pulled his head out partway, it really stretched the little asshole. When he pulled out completely, the hole gaped like a cavern. Max spat into the hole and filled it again.

Howie pounded the desk. "You're gonna ruin me! You're so fucking huge!"

Max smiled and found his rhythm again. He drove like a piston all the way in and most of the way out, faster with each stroke until Howie pounded the desk again. He withdrew his cock.

"Put it back in!"

Max smiled. "Beg for it."

"Please, sir, fuck my ass with your big cock."

Max obliged. He missed the turn once or twice and rammed into the rear of the rectum, putting pressure on Howie's bladder. Each time, Howie pissed himself a little. But he didn't complain.

"You like that?"

Howie nodded.

Max banged against the back wall rapidly a dozen times until a steady stream of urine flowed down Howie's legs, soaking his trousers. Then, when there was no more urine, Howie's little below-average penis shot a big load of cum. He hadn't touched himself. Seeing this, Max went over the edge.

"You ready, boy?"

"Yes!!!!! Fill me up!"

Max's massive balls churned. He felt the hot semen travel up his urethra for what seemed like a mile before it shot into the depths of Howie's colon. He pushed Howie onto the ground so he could let his cock drain like a garden hose after the water is turned off. Ounce after ounce of cum slowly drained from him until he was dry.

He pulled his cock out quickly, causing Howie's gaping hole to throb like a hungry mouth trying to eat bread.

"I never felt nothing like that before. Damn, that was good!"

Max grinned. "You have a beautiful ass, Howie. I'm glad you let me fuck you. But you're going to feel empty until you find someone else to fill you like I have. You won't remember me."

Howie said, "Sure, I'll remember you...uh...what was your name?" He pulled his wet pants up, marveling at the cum and piss that stained them. "Where did this come from?"

Max shrugged. "Can I have a dollar to cover the ticket to Chicago?"

Howie handed him a dollar without a second thought. When Max inspected it, he saw it was a twenty. He nearly gave it back but then decided it was payment for damages (the sign on his back) and services rendered just now.

5

THE WINDY CITY TAILOR

Next, an odd thing happened. A few minutes before the bus pulled in, Max's cock grew an inch. It was sudden. This little town was four hours from Chicago. The driver stood and adjusted himself before letting passengers in. Down his left leg was a very long penis, longer than Max's had just been. Except now, Max was a tiny bit longer than him. The driver left the bus, and a different driver came back. It was a shift change. As soon as they pulled out of the city limits, Max felt his cock shrink. A lot. He returned to the original size of barely an inch. He cursed the Devil, but when they headed into another town, his cock grew. It hurt like hell. It was perhaps nine inches and very big around now. He thought about how he had worded his wish "I want the biggest, longest, thickest dick in town...." In town. So when he was in the countryside, there were no towns. Max kept his lap covered with his coat to hide the gymnastics between his legs. He grew three inches longer in the next town but was only six inches around. The bus next passed through Fort Wayne, a small city. At the city limit sign, he was shocked when his cock nearly exploded in girth but lost two inches in length. He was maybe ten inches long. The devil always gets his due.

He figured the wish was fulfilled based on two different men in any town. One is the thickest, and one is the longest. He became both, but only just slightly. The stretching and shrinkage he felt passing through so many towns was both painful and upsetting. When the bus finally crossed the city limits into Chicago, he felt his cock swell to the thickness of bologna meat that stretched down to his mid-calf. It was obscene. He heard the disconcerting sound of his pants' seams ripping. A peek under his coat showed the tear running from his mid-thigh to his knee.

"Having trouble?" A wizened old man peered over at Max's crotch and gasped. "That's some big trouble, man."

Chicago was vast, stretching for miles in every direction. When the bus pulled in, Max stood. He hoped nobody could see what he was packing, but it was just too big. Every head turned, and women whispered in each other's ears. He was just as humiliated as he had been when his dick was small. He walked with a limp because he had grown a new leg that didn't carry its own weight. His first order of business was to find a pair of pants that fit better.

There was a tailor's shop at the far end of the busy bus depot. Max limped in and rang the bell. The tailor came out from the back. He had black hair, blue eyes, and a ruddy complexion, making him look like he was continually blushing.

"Can I help you, young man?"

Max snorted. This kid couldn't be five years older than him. "That depends. How squeamish are you?"

The tailor looked puzzled. "How do you mean?"

"I have an issue with my pants. It concerns my private parts. Intrigued or disgusted?"

The tailor smiled warmly. "Intrigued. Don't worry; I've seen a lot of strange shit here. This is the bus depot, after all."

Max let go of his jacket and let it fall to the floor, revealing the torn seam and all the flesh that caused it. "Still intrigued?"

The tailor cleared his throat. "Very. Step into my workshop." He gestured towards the back room. He took a pair of scissors and carefully cut away the pants until Max stood half naked, with his gargantuan cock dangling out the left leg of his boxer shorts.

All business, the tailor got out his measuring tape and measured Max's inseam.

"32 inches," he jotted it down.

Next, he wrapped the tape measure around the right leg in three places.

"Thigh 24 inches. Knee 12 inches. Ankle 8 inches."

The tailor hesitated. 'I'm gonna need to...'

Max was getting aroused, and it caused his third leg to swell and lengthen even more. "Do what you gotta do."

The tailor said, "I normally introduce myself to a man before I get them hard. I'm Tony."

"Tony the tailor. You need me hard?"

Tony nodded. It was impossible to know if he was blushing. "I need the maximum girth of your left leg. Do you always wear it on the left?"

Max shrugged and told a little fib. "I never noticed. The left feels natural, though."

"Just to be safe, I'm going to make both legs big enough to handle...that." The tailor licked his lips. Max sensed some desire building.

"Look to stay hard, I need to believe you're into me and want me to fuck you."

The tailor rubbed the long, thick log of flesh and kissed it up and down the length. It swelled and stretched in response. Max shivered with pleasure. The tailor took out his tape measure, never ceasing his gentle worship of Max's privates. "38 thigh, 22 knee, 8 ankle."

As soon as he had his measurements, he pulled away.

Max was confused. The man clearly wanted him. "You gonna let me fuck you?"

The tailor shook his head. "It would take someone far more talented than me to take that cock up their butt. Surely, you've never fucked anyone before? You would kill them!"

Max was taken aback. He realized he couldn't even ask the tailor to suck it. But it gently lifted away from his calves as it grew rock hard. It was so heavy that it only reached half-mast. He needed to fuck. The devil was clever.

Tony knelt and put the cock on his shoulder. He spit in his hand and rubbed the head. It felt good. Tony kept spitting and rubbing until Max was close to climax. Then he stopped. When he started again two minutes later, it felt twice as good as before. It only took a minute, and Max was ready to cum, but the tailor stopped, this time for three minutes.

"Shit, Tony, you're fucking brilliant."

Tony nodded. "I'm a fan of penises. Big, small, average - they're all so interesting. I've never seen one as big as yours." Then he spat and resumed his massage of the softball-sized cock head.

"Mmmnnnh." Max lost the power of speech as the talented tailor brought him to climax. He shot ropes of cum across the room. Tony licked the dribbling remnants. When he took Max's cock off his shoulder, it gushed a reserve of cum that had been trapped in the tunnel. It formed a thick, white puddle between his feet.

Tony got to work with his pinking shears, sewing machine, and pins. In under an hour, he had a baggy pair of pants with three large elastic loops built into both legs. Tony helped Max try on the pants, ensuring his legs passed through the loops. Once they were on, he showed him how to thread his cock under the loops and down his thigh. The result was perfect. His cock was held close to his leg. Because both pant legs were baggy, it perfectly camouflaged the monstrous log of flesh. He walked around the shop, pleased with how comfortable the pants were.

"Tony, you're a genius. What do I owe you?"

Tony punched a few keys on the adding machine. "$14.75."

Max panicked. He only had about nineteen dollars and needed to stay at a hotel tonight.

"Can I give you half and come back tomorrow?"

Tony nodded. Max peeled off a five and three ones. "I'll come back tomorrow with the other half."

Tony got a glazed look in his eye. "Hello, sir. Can I help you with anything?"

Max knew this would happen, but he had no idea how much it could hurt. He had formed an intimate bond with Tony. He wanted a friend. But Tony didn't remember him anymore. It was painful.

Max smiled through the pain. "Yes, I got off a bus, and I'm looking for a good place to hang my hat for a week. Can you recommend anything?"

Tony said, "That depends. What's your budget?"

Max had about eleven dollars left if he had counted right. "I dunno. Ten dollars for a week?"

Tony sucked his teeth. "You're going to have to stay at the Central YMCA on Lasalle with that kind of money."

Max shrugged. He just wanted to sleep.

6

YOUNG MAN'S CHRISTIAN ASSOCIATION

Tony pointed him down the street to LaSalle. The "Y" was a bit grungy. Max didn't mind. He had somewhere to stay for a week. They gave him a room on the 11th floor with a spectacular view of Downtown. As he walked to his room, he noticed many doors were open. Curious, he poked his head into one of the open rooms. A red-headed young man lay on his stomach, his bare ass in the air. He motioned him in.

There was a code of silence. He unbuttoned Max's pants, but when he saw the monster lurking inside, he broke the code.

"Holy Shit! I can't do that. I'm sorry, man."

Max shrugged and turned to leave. The young man said, "Room 1113 is a fister. He can handle you."

Max was tired but also intrigued. Fucking Howie with his great big cock had been very satisfying, but he couldn't imagine how good it would feel to put this monster inside someone. He put his hand on it just to be sure. It was like trying to hold a coffee can. His fingers spread as far as they could but didn't reach halfway. This really could kill someone. But 1113 beckoned.

The door was open, and a thick, hairy, muscle man was just finishing up inside the boyish blond man who lay prostrate on his bed. His eyes lit up when Max walked into the room.

"Almost done here." As if on cue, the man on top groaned and spread himself to cover the boy with his big frame. "Oh! I'm coming. I'm coming." Max could hear the sperm shooting into the boy. He watched the man's big balls pump like a bee stinger.

After a few more tender kisses and nibbles on the ear, the hulking man pulled out and stood. The boy let out a fart that sounded like a Bronx cheer. In any normal world, the hairy man would be considered well-hung. It was maybe eight inches and relatively thick. It had a nice swing to it.

The man walked over and gently hit him on the shoulder. "It's like throwing a hot dog down a hallway." He left the room completely naked and entered another one with its door ajar.

The supine boy on the bed lay on his side, looking at Max. "Those pants reveal nothing. I have to warn you; I like them big. If you're small, I'll send you packing."

The part of Max who remembered Rowan, his small self, was insulted and disgusted. But Max was ready to give this boy what he wanted. He was thin, but his buttocks were very round and firm.

"I have a feeling you won't be disappointed." Max unbuckled his trousers and let them drop. The elastic loops prevented the pants from falling to the floor. Instead, the top of his cock was exposed. The boy's eyes widened. Just the few inches that were exposed were shocking.

"Are you part mule?" The boy's eyes glittered with anticipation.

"Only the devil knows."

When the boy presented his ass, Max noticed how similar it looked to the volcanic anus he fucked in the forest the day before. "Looks loose."

The boy grinned proudly. "It's the loosest ass North of the Mason-Dixon line."

Max guffawed. "I like it."

The boy made eye contact. "Watch this." He bore down like he was taking a turd, and a bright cherry-red knot of flesh pushed its way out like a giant apple. The boy squeezed his anus, and the whole thing disappeared as quickly as it had appeared.

"It's called a rosebud. Beautiful, isn't it?"

Max nodded. He struggled to get out of his pants because he had gotten very hard very fast when that rosebud popped out.

At last, bent over at the waist, he got them off. When he straightened, he revealed his swollen, throbbing meat. The boyish man blanched.

"Oh no, honey, that is too big! I think. Come over here and give it a try."

The boy's anus had the same volcanic shape. It was as if the devil had possessed him. "How did your ass get like that?"

"I let men put big things up my ass. Not just dicks. Arms, legs, whatever will fit."

Max wanted to be disgusted, but it turned him on even more. "Well, I know this isn't as big as a leg, at least." Max pushed his cock into the boy. It wasn't anything like a hot dog in a hallway, but it was definitely like a kielbasa in a mail chute. He buried himself to the hilt in less than a minute, with not even a single cry of pain from the loose boy. He groaned a few times, but the noises expressed pleasure, not discomfort or pain.

"Fill me up!!! Oh God, fill me up!" The blond was biting his pillow.

"That's all I got."

"Push harder!"

With a light pop, his head left the sigmoid colon and climbed the descending colon. The boy began to spasm.

"Am I hurting you?"

The boy shook his head but said nothing. His pants and moans expressed joy. The boy kept spasming. Max grew worried. But then he felt the boy's tortured guts caress his dick. The insides of the boy were pumping like that bee-stinger ball sac. This boy was having an orgasm! In his ass!

Max plowed him long and deep. The boy took every inch without complaint. It was what he imagined it would feel like to fuck a pussy. The insides were slick with cum from a dozen men. He slid and sloshed about. Max put a hand on the boy's penis, which was tiny. He slapped it away.

Soon, Max felt the gurgling rising in his balls. He stopped for a minute, letting the climax subside before it happened. He continued to fuck for another two minutes, then stopped again. He was taking what Tony had taught him and putting it to use.

When he finally ejaculated, it was a nonstop torrent of cum.

"Oh fuck, man, your cum is on fire! It's so hot!"

Indeed, Max felt an infernal heat in his climax. Because of the angle of entry, he shot it all, and hardly any cum was left to drain out.

He pulled out in a swift motion. The boy let out a silent fart through the giant opening in his butt. He stood, unaware of the stream of cum pouring out of his ass.

"Holy fuck. That was the best yet. You gave me an orgasm! It's been years since I felt full enough to have one. Oh god, I'll never forget you. How will anything compare? I'll never be satisfied again."

Max smiled. "You'll forget all about me when I walk out of here." He picked up his pants and strolled naked down the hallway to his room.

7

THE OLDEST PROFESSION

Two weeks later, Max Andrews was strapped for cash. He wasn't able to earn it like normal folks. The hiring manager wouldn't recognize him at the end of the day, so he wouldn't get paid. He could rob a bank. They wouldn't be able to describe who did it. But he didn't want to get shot by a heroic security guard. He was hungry. He stole a sandwich from a cart. The man saw him but forgot why he was angry.

Max walked East until he came to the Elevated Railway or "The L." He hopped over the turnstile. He heard yelling, but it didn't last. Nobody noticed him, or if they did, they didn't remember.

He caught the first train south. Elegant tall buildings gave way to well-kept row houses, which gave way to slums. He didn't want to get off, but it was getting worse. He got off in the district called "The Levee." In the days when Chicago was the western frontier, The Levee was home to saloons and brothels. Nowadays, it was just a popular spot for streetwalkers.

Max didn't feel safe until he found a different kind of alley. It smelled of leather and after-shave. Men stood with one leg against the wall, nodding to the cars passing by. Max was intrigued. He watched a pretty young boy lean into a Rolls Royce Phantom. He overheard the boy say, "Seventy-five up front," before hopping in. The beautiful car sped off, turned right, and disappeared.

One man with an unfortunate face compared to his perfect, muscled body said, "Hey, kid. C'mere."

Max knew the guy wouldn't remember him for long, so he didn't sense any real danger. He extended his hand. "Hello. Max."

"I'm Bones. Hey guy, what are you selling?"

"I beg your pardon?"

"You ain't advertising right. You don't wear baggy pants." The hustler pointed to his own tight blue jeans. There was a sizable lump in his crotch. "I'm selling dick. You selling dick or ass? You gotta lean with your right leg up if you're selling ass."

Max was about to clear up the misunderstanding but the foggy look washed over Bones's face. Max walked away. He had gathered a lot of information in a very short time. He needed money. Running grifts was tiresome. This looked more fun. He picked a spot on the wall and raised his left foot. He tightened the pant leg revealing a hint of what lurked beneath. Heads swiveled. He heard a few wolf whistles, and then he turned invisible again.

A Plymouth slowed and stopped. Inside, a well-dressed banker-type motioned him over. Max sauntered up to the passenger window. "Yeah?"

"Is that real?" He pointed at Max's left leg. Max nodded. The man wanted it. Max could tell.

"Eighty-five up front." The man shrugged. Max hopped in. The man immediately put a hand on Max's monster cock.

"Holy wow!"

Max cleared his throat. "Eighty-five."

The man fished his wallet from his blazer and gave Max two fifties. "Keep the change." They were parked on a dark street. The man kneeled on the driver's seat, his head poking out of the open window. He lowered his pants, revealing a gaping anus. Why hadn't this guy forgotten him yet?

The man looked back at Max. "I wanted another go." His face sharpened. It was Barbax.

Max smacked his forehead. "Oh shit."

The demon cackled, then said, "Nope. Clean and tidy."

Max was too perplexed to be disgusted by Barbax's poop joke. In truth, Max hadn't figured out how to fuck someone since his lucky night in 1113. Had that boy been Barbax, too? No, the demon was too vain not to reveal himself. With the inviting, gaping ass so readily available to fuck, he figured it wouldn't hurt to go a second round.

There aren't many sex positions possible in a Plymouth, especially not in the front seat. Barbax stretched out face down. Max lay on top of him, his ass raised to the ceiling. His cock was still trapped in the middle of the demon's back. He leaned back until his bare ass pressed against the passenger window. He had to wait for his cock to soften before he could bend the end and enter the devil's ass.

The sex was good, but not great. The devil enjoyed it much more than Max. Unable to move or shift positions, Max kept humping until he came. Even with two weeks' worth of cum, it was just a dribble.

"You're pretty fucking huge, Max. You should go to Los Angeles if you want to feel it dragging on the ground. An aspiring blond actor can't get a job there because his dick's even bigger than yours."

"I'd rip my pants on Route 66."

The demon howled. "Oh man, I'm clever! That was one of my finest tricks. It rips your pants? He gestured to Max's baggy trousers."

Max said, "Well, not these."

The demon was in stitches, thoroughly amused at Max's expense. "Trust me, Max; you're gonna love Los Angeles. Now get back to work so you can buy an airplane ticket!"

Max hadn't thought of that. Flying over a town, maybe he wouldn't stretch and shrink so much. But Chicago was a cool place. Why ever would he go to Los Angeles? In a few months, he would know that answer.

8

TAILORED FOR MAXIMUM EFFECT

With Barbax's hundred bucks, Max paid a month at the Y and visited his train station tailor. The tailor didn't remember him but was happy to make a custom suit that accentuated his best asset. Before he could take out a tape measure, Max handed him the paper with his measurements from the last time.

"Your handwriting looks just like mine."

Max grinned. "I'll bet you're into dick."

The tailor nodded. "How did you know?"

Max said, "I'm a little clairvoyant."

The tailor said, "Is there a huge cock in my future?"

Max paused. "That depends. Do a good job, and I might reward you."

Made of light khaki-colored worsted wool, the suit pants had elastic in the vertical seams. This meant the lightweight fabric held his cock in place but left nothing to the imagination. Max tried them on. He had paid the tailor up front in case he forgot him. He hadn't.

"Take off the pants so I can...iron them."

Max kept the handsome blazer on but stripped from the waist down. His massive cock rocked back and forth like a pendulum. He handed the pants to the tailor, who couldn't keep his eyes off the colossal prize hanging before him.

The tailor said, "Funny. Deja vu."

Max didn't know the French phrase. He studied German in school. "Day what?"

"Deja vu. When I look at your cock, I feel like I've seen it before. But I have never seen one anywhere near this size."

Max shrugged. "Maybe you just don't remember."

The tailor shook his head. "No, it's just my mind playing tricks on me."

The tailor kneeled to find his iron under the counter. Max put his cock over the man's shoulder. "Don't you want to rub one out?"

"I can't possibly let you fuck me." The tailor looked up into Max's stern face.

"I'd settle for a hand job. Use lots of spit."

The tailor frowned. "It's like you know me."

Max said, "Remember, I'm clairvoyant."

The tailor ironed with one hand and warmed up his customer with the other. He polished the head. His smooth hands had never known hard work. It made Max's knees buckle. He grabbed the counter.

"Wait till you get both hands. I'm almost done here." He continued to rub vigorously where the foreskin connected to the head. Max was really sensitive there. He always had been. Some things don't change with size.

Tony the Tailor handed Max his pants, folded and wrinkle-free. "Come back any time if you need an adjustment. Now, let me try something."

The tailor turned and stepped back a foot or so. Max's cock was so heavy that the poor man groaned like a weightlifter with a 75-pound dumbbell. He clamped his mouth over the tip, using his tongue to tickle the sensitive area. At the same time, he used both hands to almost encircle the beast. He spat repeatedly until it was slippery. He let his mouth do most of the work, but he did run his hands slowly up and down the length of Max's meat.

Max felt better in Tony's hands than he had fucking the devil's bottomless pit. The tailor was tender and careful. He worshipped Max's cock like it was his lord. He knelt in obeisance to the almighty dick. Seeing the devotion in Tony's eyes and movements, Max got really turned on.

"Yeah, just like that. Keep going." Max was getting close. The tailor could sense this and picked up speed, his hands running up and down ever faster like a masturbatory "Halva Nagila." Max felt even more powerful than he had in room 1113. This tailor worshipped him.

"Goddamn, man, I'm gonna come."

The tailor didn't stop. He looked up at Max like a parishioner praying, eyes full of love and devotion. Max couldn't take it another second.

"Shit! Shit! Oh, man!" He fired a warm round of cum into the tailor's mouth. The tailor caught every drop. Max fired again and again until some of his cum came out of the tailor's nose.

"Swallow it."

Tony looked up at Max and obeyed him. He stood, letting the heavy deflating cock fall. He kissed Max, and his mouth tasted of cum. Max stared into his eyes, feeling the first stirrings of something more than just sex. Then Tony's eyes clouded over.

"Who the fuck are you? Why are you naked? Get out of here!"

Max grabbed his new pants and his older baggy pair and ran from the shop onto a crowded platform. All eyes turned to him. He did his best to cover himself from the front, but it was hopeless. The big slab of meat kept peeking out.

A woman fainted. A policeman's whistle blew. Max

put the pants under his arms and ran. There was a policeman between him and the bathroom.

"Please, sir, I had an accident."

He tried to escape the policeman's grip but wasn't nimble enough. His cock hit the cop's leg with a loud 'thwap!'

"Hold it right there!" The cop slapped a handcuff on Max and another on his own wrist.

"Officer, please."

"Put on your fucking pants."

Max chose the baggy pair, not wanting to attract any more attention. The cop grabbed his cock and pulled on it.

"You hiding any weapons in that thing?"

Max said, "No, sir."

The officer walked him to his car and undid the cuffs.

"Get in!"

Max hesitated. He looked into the officer's eyes, which were growing cloudy.

"Officer, can you tell me how to get to North Canal?"

The cop shook his head to clear the clouds. "North Canal? You're gonna walk right up Clinton to Lake, make a right, and it starts one block over on the left."

"Thank you, officer. You be safe."

"You too, mister."

9

THE ACCOUNTANT

The khaki wool pants were a big moneymaker for Max. It was hot out, and the traffic on that alley was constant. Everyone stopped to look at Max. He walked down to the car and said, "Eighty-five up front. I won't get in the car unless you pay me." It worked. The men paid him, and he would climb in. He was still on the grift, but this was so lucrative; he had to keep it up. He took money from priests, proctologists, lawyers, and judges. They would drive down to the dark parking lot, and Max would say, "Let's do this outside."

Some men protested, but Max just stepped out of the car and pulled out his dick to lure them. Most of these men worshipped Max, but none could do much more than jerk themselves off. Usually, right after they came, they would forget him. He'd walk away, leaving them wondering what had just happened.

One night, a nervous accountant let on that he was into fisting. Max figured he'd give the man his money's worth. The accountant dropped his pants in the parking lot, showing a loose hole. Max didn't think it was stretchy enough, but the man insisted. He was already clean and lubricated. Max wished the guy would remember the fuck of a lifetime, but he wouldn't.

Max hadn't been inside someone's ass since the last time Barbax paid him a visit. It was so familiar that he forgot that the guy was in over his head. He pushed his way in, and the accountant let out a blood-curdling scream.

Max backed out, but the accountant said, "Don't mind me. I'm loud."

"I don't want to hurt you, man."

"I want you to."

Max shrugged and shoved his cock back inside the hole. It was looser than before. He pushed his way through the man, hoping the screams wouldn't bring cops. The cops didn't give a shit about anyone in the Levee; nobody showed up. A few neighbors shouted, "Shut up!"

The accountant, Bernie, was surprisingly capable once he got used to Max inside him. He rode the cock himself, back and forth, leaving snail trails on the base of Max's thick pole. Bernie was light, and Max was strong. He picked Bernie up and carried him around the parking lot playing "Ride-a-Horsey." Bernie bounced with abandon. Max saw a massive bulge moving up and down in Bernie's skinny abdomen. That huge lump was Max. It was an incredible turn-on. Bernie wasn't handsome or strong. He was passionate. That, combined with the sight of his cock underneath Bernie's skin, was enough to bring Max to climax.

Bernie shot his load first without touching himself. Max was impressed. Bernie came in great volumes, rivaling Max. In a touching moment, Bernie kissed Max while his ass filled with cum. It was a surprise.

After the kiss, Bernie looked up at his strong protector.

"Who are you? Owww! Owww!"

Bernie pulled away and fell off Max's cock, landing on his back. He screamed, but he had already cried wolf. No one cared. Max ran off, a hundred dollars richer. It didn't make the sting of lost passion smart any less.

10

FLIGHT FROM WINTER

Winter came in like a wailing banshee at a symphony. Chicago was covered in snow, and the air outside was so cold you could die if you stayed outside. Max read the newspaper, forecasting seven below zero in Chicago. In the National forecast, Los Angeles was a sunny 73. He remembered the demon's words. He had enough money from his prostitution to afford a plane ticket and a few months' rent in a clean, safe boarding house. He listened to the other men selling their bodies and overheard many interesting things. Every big city had male prostitutes. Los Angeles more than any other. The movie business attracted handsome men like flies.

Unable to stand another minute of the windy frozen winter, Max called Boeing Air and booked a flight to Los Angeles. Max shrunk rapidly when the wheels lifted off the pavement until his penis was the same tiny worm he'd had just before he met Barbax. He wasn't in any town, so he went back to default. At the same time, he felt all the energy flow out of him. He felt like he had the flu or was a junkie withdrawing from heroin. The plane couldn't travel the 1,500 miles, so it made three stops. The first was in Cedar Rapids. The moment the wheels touched down, Max felt his cock grow to a manageable size. It was perhaps nine inches and very thick. Some of the energy returned, but Max was still shaky.

After takeoff, he grew pale and sweaty. The woman sitting across from him tapped his shoulder.

"Hi, I didn't see you there. Are you okay?"

Max wasn't okay, but it was temporary. Their next stop was Denver. There had to be a monster there somewhere. "I'm just a little air sick."

"Here," she handed him a wax-paper bag. "If you need to vomit, do it in the bag."

Max was helpless to bring back the lost sense of power coursing through his veins. The woman turned to him. "Hey, are you okay? You look sick."

Max nodded. He held up the waxed paper bag.

When the wheels touched down in Denver, Max nearly screamed from the pain as his cock ballooned into a thick, past-the-knee cock. The rush of power was incredible. He moaned softly, disturbing the passengers around him, who had no idea what he was going through. They forgot him moments later.

The plane had to refuel in Denver, so they would be there for a while. Max wanted to pee now that he had a cock that could get close to the toilet. The steward had posted a sign "Please don't use restroom between touchdown and takeoff." He couldn't wait. With a glance over either shoulder, he entered the tiny restroom. It was little more than an outhouse. Max took out the cock. It was as big around as a soup can and rested on his knee as he pissed. Max thought he could live with a cock like this. He'd get laid a lot more. Maybe have kids someday with a woman. Then the thought of being with a woman left him feeling queasy. His big cock was meant to be shared with another man. He realized he was a faggot, just like Jeff had assumed back in Defiance. A banging on the door startled him out of his thoughts.

"Mister, you just pissed on the engineer's head! Get out of there now!"

FLIGHT ATTENDANT
FROM HELL

Absentmindedly, Max opened the door. The steward was handsome, like Douglas Fairbanks. His eyes bugged out at the sight of Max's modest, manageable monster.

Max knew this flight attendant was in the big dick appreciation club. He pulled him into the john by the bow tie. The door locked behind him.

"What are you into?"

The flight attendant smirked. "I like fucking guys with big ones."

"You want me to fuck you, right?"

The attendant shook his head. Max saw he wore a name tag that read 'Orobas.'

"You don't?" Max was puzzled until he felt something throbbing against his crotch. A light went on. "You want to fuck me."

The attendant took out a tube of Vaseline. "You want it?"

Max didn't want it, but something compelled him. He bent at the hips, revealing his hairy ass. A cold finger covered with lubricant worked its way into his virgin hole.

"Can I at least see what you're working with, Orobas?"

The attendant said, "I could have you arrested for pissing on the tarmac. Now shut up and take it like the bitch you are."

Max was surprised at how turned on he was by the vulgar language. He wanted to be fucked. A searing hot pain ripped through him when Orobas inserted the tip of his penis. Max reached back to try to feel its size, but the attendant slapped his hand.

"I've never done this before."

"I know." Orobas forced his way in a little further. The pain was blinding.

"How do you know?"

"I know a virgin hole when I see one." With that, he shoved hard. The head popped in, followed by a long shaft. It felt alive inside Max like a serpent was crawling in his guts.

Max's cock smacked against the vanity with each violent thrust from Orobas. He forgot the pain. "Don't. Stop."

The attendant snickered. "I won't."

Max felt incredible relief, letting go, letting someone else be the man. How could it feel this good?

"It doesn't. Not normally." Orobas had read his mind. He turned his head back to see Barbax grinning as he plowed into Max.

"Oh yeah, I forgot to tell you. If anyone says they want to fuck you, neither have any choice. You'll let that man fuck you. It's all included in the deal."

Max wanted to be angry, but the demon's cock in his ass felt too good.

"It's so fucking good!"

Barbax slapped Max on the ass. "I'm the best there is. You'll be chasing this feeling for the rest of your life!"

Max felt his insides twitching. They spasmed. His whole body was shaking with what he would describe as a dry orgasm. As he shook, Orobas grunted. "Oh yeah, man, keep twitching."

Max had no choice. He was in full anal orgasm. He realized now why Barbax's cock felt like a serpent. It probably was. The long cock wriggled inside him. It began to swell, stretching his hole more and more. Max reached behind to feel the girth. He couldn't get his fingers all the way around. It should have hurt, but it felt like being owned. He belonged to Barbax.

The passive role suited Max far better than the active one. If a guy was too afraid to let Max fuck him, Max could offer up his ass. That turned him on so much that he reached climax.

"I'm gonna come!" Max didn't care who heard. Nobody but Barbax would remember him in a minute. His thick cock, pressed against the vanity, grew a little thicker just before he shot his load. His shoes were ruined.

The demon held Max by the hips. "I could do this for hours, but we're about to take off."

His serpentine cock thrashed and wriggled and spat out a scorching load of cum in Max's burning gut.

Barbax leaned against Max, breathing hard. "I tell you what. I'll make sure every fuck feels almost that good for your partner. And for you. No matter what."

Max turned to say something, but he was gone.

The plane rocketed down the runway. Max had to sit down hard on the toilet. When the nose pointed up, Max looked down. His cock was shriveling and pulling back to his pubic mound. Soon it looked like a large nipple or a clitoris. Max didn't miss seeing that. It was humiliating.

When the plane touched down outside Flagstaff, Max saw no change in his cock. He felt weak, but the Devil's cum was like a Dr. Pepper for his weakness. It kept him going. The airport was outside the city limits, and nobody lived there. Max passed out in his seat, waking to the sunrise over California.

12

THE CITY OF ANGELS

The plane landed safely at Glendale Airport. Max, however, didn't feel safe, knowing Barbax could jump him any time. He went from a nipple to a baby's arm holding an apple. He was puzzled at first. It was enormous, but it was dwarfed by what he had possessed in Chicago and Denver. Then he saw the sign: "The Grand Central Air Terminal and City of Glendale welcome you to Los Angeles." He wasn't in Los Angeles yet. He caught a taxi to the Pacific Electric car headed towards Central Station. Between Lomita and Los Feliz, his cock shrank again to the tiny nub he hated with all his heart. They were in an unincorporated area with no residents. Then they crossed the Los Angeles city limits.

Max went from a nipple to a rolled carpet. The pain was excruciating. All the passengers around him screamed as the most monstrous cock yet swelled up in his baggy pants and pushed its way to his ankles. Barbax had warned him about the guy here who was gigantic. There must have been another fellow whose cock was as thick as a large tin can of tomatoes. After the passengers had scattered, they forgot he was there or why they were sitting so close together at one end of the car. Max heaved a sigh of relief. After Edendale, they entered a tunnel and came out at Central Station.

The sheer volume of his cock made it nearly impossible for Max to get to his feet. There was no way to hide his deformity. He could only wait for the people around him to forget him. Using a pole for leverage, he managed to go from sitting to standing. Carefully, he exited the train. He walked like he had lumbago. People stared and then turned away. He made no eye contact. He managed to walk up Stanford to 4th, where he saw a small hotel. He couldn't walk much further until he got used to the enormous weight between his legs.

The front desk clerk at the Aster was unfriendly, contrary to all Max had heard about the Sunshine State. He took one look at Max's torn pants and exposed penis.

"Get the fuck outta here. May the Lord smite you!"

Max tried to remain polite.

"Can you recommend another hotel nearby?"

The guy turned away. He had already forgotten Max. Max had done this before. He used the payphone in the lobby.

"I need to rent a room for an entire month. Can you do that?"

"For a reservation like that, I need two weeks up front. No can do."

"I have a man on the ground in Los Angeles. He will bring you the cash. You give him the keys."

The clerk took out a pen. "Name?"

"Andrews. Max Andrews."

The clerk scribbled notes on his desk blotter. "Okay, that's twelve dollars up front."

"My man will be there shortly."

Max waited until the clerk had turned away. He sidled to the front counter, hiding his pudendum from the pious jerk.

"I got an envelope from Max Andrews."

The clerk scratched his head. "I don't know about no Max Andrews, buddy."

Max pointed to the blotter. "Jog your memory?"

"I don't remember writing this; hang on." The clerk studied his handwriting, clearly puzzled. "Okay, it says twelve dollars now, and then I gotta give you the keys."

Before the clerk could forget him, Max got the key to a room on the second floor. He took back his twelve dollars without the clerk noticing. The room had a view of the vast nothingness that was Los Angeles. Searchlights lit up the sky at theaters where the latest talking picture was premiering. Max had a fleabag bed to sleep in, and that was enough. He could figure out how to cover himself properly in the morning. He took off his pants and slept nude, using his massive penis as a side pillow.

13

TOO BIG FOR HIS BRITCHES

Max awoke refreshed after his many hours of travel. The sky outside was gray, and the air smelled of the ocean. Max stood before the cracked mirror, surveying his situation. Two inches of his cock were exposed because the massive head had torn the cuffs. He just needed to let out the cuffs, strap himself in, and he might look normal. For now, he tied a bandana around his ankle. Entering and exiting little hotels like this one was always tricky. The best thing for him to do was to walk through the lobby at top speed and exit before the clerk got a good look at him. Outside on the sidewalk, he turned to see the clerk chasing him. The clerk came out and stood next to Max. "Hey, did you see?"

"See what, sir?"

The guy shook his head. "I gotta quit drinking so late."

Max didn't have to walk far to find a tailor. He strolled up 4th Street towards Broadway, passing a bank, a jeweler, a palm reader, and a hat maker to get to Town Tailors. The grouch behind the counter was old and world-weary. "What can I do you for?"

Max shrugged. "I have an extremely embarrassing situation."

"I've seen everything. This is Los Angeles. What did you shit your pants?"

Max laughed. "No, I-- well, it's best if I show you."

Max put his left leg on the platform, removing his bandana.

The tailor tried to hide his astonishment. "Okay, you surprised me with something new."

"I can't explain why, but these pants used to fit, and now they're just too tight."

The tailor asked him to remove his trousers, pulling the curtain around for modesty. Max feared the tailor would forget him if he were out of sight. He pulled the curtain open to talk. "Oh, hey, what can you do?"

"I'm going to put a knickerbocker style of button in both hems, sewn to an elastic band to allow a little give."

Max loved the idea. He had to keep the tailor talking, or he'd be run out of the shop naked.

"I hope you don't mind. I like to talk."

The tailor grunted because his mouth was full of pins.

Max continued, "I just flew here from Chicago."

"Flew?" The tailor let a few pins fall. "In an aeroplane?"

"Yessir. I landed at Grand Central Air Terminal yesterday."

The tailor picked up the pins. "Was it scary?"

Max thought about his painful landings and enervating takeoffs. "Yeah, in a way. I think everybody reacts differently when they fly."

Max had grown very good at small talk since it was the only way to beat Barbax's curse. The tailor finished the modifications to the trousers.

"Try these on."

Max closed the curtain, taking a while to thread himself into the pants. To his relief, he could slip the monster through the loops. The buttons on the elasticated hem were just right. If he needed to tighten, there were two extra button holes.

When Max opened the curtain, the tailor jumped. "How did you get there?"

Max wanted to pay the man, but he couldn't. He walked out. When he turned back, the tailor shook his head and turned his head sideways, pounding on his temple like he was trying to get a bug out of his ear.

❧ 14 ❧
THE STRIP

With renewed confidence, Max caught a Western Division streetcar to Hollywood. Nobody noticed his deformity. The tailor had done an excellent job. Hollywood was bustling. There were a dozen movie studios crammed into the small neighborhood. Everywhere you looked, there was an aspiring actress or a handsome model. Max turned a few heads. He was a rather handsome lad himself. Nobody seemed to notice that he carried thirty pounds of cock in his pants. They probably thought he had a wooden leg, or maybe they didn't think anything at all. The less impression he made, the more quickly he disappeared from their minds.

Max wasn't able or interested in being an actor. Nobody knew him long enough to put him in a moving picture, which took many days to make. He grew bored with Hollywood and hopped back on the train bound for Santa Monica. That was a mistake. The second the car crossed Crescent Heights, Max shrank back to nipple size. West of Hollywood lay an unincorporated part of the city called Sherman. It was much more exciting than Hollywood. There were topless bars, gangster restaurants, lurid hotel rooms, and even a little street prostitution. He hopped off at the County Strip, as it was known. He felt relieved to be so small for a while. Flappers and booze hounds drove by in jalopies, hooting and howling like animals. It was the most exciting place Max had ever been. And while he was here, he didn't have the heavy burden. It was a relief to be free of Barbax's spell for a while.

A female prostitute came up to him. "Very clever."

"I beg your pardon?" Max wasn't used to being addressed. People rarely noticed him.

"I said, very clever, to hide out on the Strip. But you must know, my influence here is greater than anywhere else in the sinful city of angels."

The prostitute had an annoying goatee. It was Barbax. He had followed him here.

The demon continued. "My bargains are ironclad. You can't get out of it. Not here, not anywhere."

Max said, "I think I heard about people getting out of your contracts before."

The demon said, "Impossible. If you think Orpheus won, you're a fool. He lost the love of his life."

Max shook his head. "I was thinking about the peasant who sold the Devil his crops above ground, but he planted turnips."

Barbax blanched. "How do you know about that?"

Max laughed. "It's in Grimm's Fairy Tales, you illiterate demon."

Barbax was obviously shaken. But he put on his smug grin again. "You didn't make such a bargain with me, so I'm not worried in the least."

Max didn't know how to outsmart the demon...yet. He vowed to go to the library and read up on those Rumpelstiltskin-style "fool-the-devil" stories. He was sure something in the contract rendered it null and void. He would know eventually.

Max stayed on the County Strip for several days, securing a bungalow at the Chateau Marmont. A brand new, magnificent Spanish-style hotel, the Chateau Marmont loomed over the County Strip. By the pool were the bungalows. Max was in the pool every day, enjoying having nothing between his legs again. He used his ass to lure well-hung gentlemen to his spot. They stretched his hole, dumped their load, and promptly forgot who he was.

15
DANTE'S HOLE

Max discovered something troubling. The city line must have crossed the property at the northernmost part of the pool. Max found out when he seduced a handsome hairy Italian man with a mustache. He had a nice large cock, and was particularly interested in playing with Max's tiny penis. He had his hand down Max's swimsuit, stroking him, biting his neck. Suddenly, his minuscule cock began to swell and stretch most painfully. Max was in a panic. He wasn't sure what had caused it. The man stepped back and watched in horror as the monster forced its way out of the woolen suit. It bobbed on the water, floating like a dead body. The man shrieked in terror, causing the bellhops to come running. Max leaped forward, covering his cock with his body. He drifted south. The massive cock turned into a tiny nipple again. The man he'd been playing with introduced himself again. "Dante. And you are?"

Max made sure to stay away from that end of the pool. The mustached man tickled his neck and put a meaty finger in Max's ass.

Max smiled. "My place or yours?"

The man was semi-hard. Max's tiny penis was a huge turn-on to him. "I can't get out of the pool just yet."

Dante gestured towards his big almost-hard Italian cock, which refused to deflate.

It was a Tuesday, but a couple of starlets and a smattering of producers were still lying out in the December sun.

"My bungalow is right there." Max pointed. He knew if they got separated, he would have to start over. Max took the man's hand and practically yanked him out of the water. The man put his hand on his modestly huge penis and ran with Max to the adorable cottage.

Max lay with his legs in the air, savoring the feeling of having almost nothing between his legs. Dante licked and sucked Max's miniature meat.

"This, it is so adorable." Dante pointed to Max's little thing. The man moved his mustache south to Max's butthole. He used his fingers to stimulate Max, who was at risk of climaxing before the fun had started. Max grabbed his wrist and moved the offending hand down to his asshole. Dante needed no further prompting. He put one, two, three fingers inside Max. Max was surprised by just how thick the man's fingers were. Then he got a better look at Dante's big Italian cock. Dante hadn't been anywhere near erect in the pool. This was the thickest cock he'd ever seen besides his own.

"I have to put my hand in you to make you stretch." Max nodded. He had secured a little bottle of cocaine from a starlet who handed it to him just before he walked away. He took a tiny sniff, and the universe went numb. He felt Dante's greased hand enter him fully. He felt Dante pull out and punch his way in a dozen times. Max was ready for the Italian stallion.

"This might hurt." Dante pushed into Max, who indeed felt a great deal of pain. One more sniff of the cocaine sent him to a snowy mountaintop where pain held no sway over his body. Inch by inch, Dante explored Max's inferno with his club-like cock. Max yielded, letting him pass into the sacred spot where the rectum ends, and the colon begins. It made several loud pops as the hairy man worked his way deeper. For one horrible moment, Max was afraid it was Barbax in disguise. But the Devil would have revealed himself by now and certainly wouldn't have forgotten him in the pool. He sighed and allowed pleasure to bombard him.

Dante worked the little nub between Max's legs until the young man couldn't hold back. He shot a massive load on Dante's furry chest.

"So much cum from such a little penis. Oh, Dio! I'm gonna come too. Dante pounded Max hard, building up friction along the length of his extremely fat cock. Max could feel the cock pull back on its own before spewing a torrent of cum in his asshole. Dante collapsed in a sweaty heap. Max went to get a washcloth. When he came back, Dante looked confused.

"This isn't my room. Where am I?"

Max had turned this into a game in Chicago. "You hit your head diving into the pool. I rescued you."

Dante's eyes dipped down to Max's package. "Oh, I like them small like that!"

"I'll be right back." Max went back into the bathroom and locked the door. When he came out five minutes later, Dante was gone.

16

HONOR AMONG THIEVES

There were several illegal gambling halls on the Strip. Max cruised the tables, looking for stray poker chips. Security often came running, but he would turn away, and they forgot what they were chasing. He was able to secure several thousand dollars in a very short time. He could buy a house if the realtor would remember him. No, this was living money. Money to buy things under glass or otherwise difficult to obtain legally.

Max missed his enormous cock. He missed knocking things over with it. He missed the reassuring feeling just above his ankle where the head rubbed. It was time to go back inside the city. He gave his bungalow one last loving stare before he left. Some of the best sex he had was underneath the men at that place. He didn't need a big dick. Nobody could take it, anyway. But he yearned for that feeling again. Being small was much better than he imagined. When he made his bargain, he didn't yet know he would enjoy sex as a passive homosexual. He had still been focused on a wife, three children, and a house with a picket fence. The moment he let go of that illusion, all the pleasure in the world was his to enjoy. "Besides," he told himself, "I couldn't get a woman pregnant with this little thing."

The streetcar continued down Sunset before cutting down to Santa Monica Boulevard. When he crossed Doheny, his cock swelled and stretched to the size and shape of a large salami. It wasn't the long cock he expected. Then he saw the sign. "Beverly Hills."

The car passed through a quaint shopping district. Wealthy movie stars lived here, so the shops catered to a more cultivated crowd than the people on the Strip. Max got off the trolley so he could adjust his trousers to accommodate the unwieldy cock. He entered I. Magnin department store and made a beeline for the men's room. He wasn't prepared for what he saw there.

It was like a Hieronymus Bosch painting. Sucking and fucking brazenly, the men behaved like animals. When they saw Max's massive bulge, they descended on him like rats on a corpse. He locked himself in a toilet stall. Fists pounded, then stopped. They forgot him. But Max had to be careful. There was the other part of his blessing/curse that if a man said he wanted to fuck him, he would have no choice. Luckily, no one had said it out loud just yet.

Max put the long thick cock into his elastic loops. It almost reached his knee. When he was sure he was well camouflaged, he opened the door and ran out of the bathroom. A men's watch caught his eye as he passed the jewelry counter. It was made by Piaget. He wanted a watch like that. It was a hundred dollars. His pilfered money burned a hole in his pocket, so he bought the watch before the counter girl forgot who he was. It felt good to really purchase something. Stealing was no fun anymore.

❧ 17 ❧

THE COUNTRY CLUB

To get to the tiny seaside town of Santa Monica, Max would have to cross into Westwood and Brentwood, two neighborhoods of Los Angeles. He thought it best not to take a streetcar, so he could find a strategic place to make the transition. Beverly Hills ended at the Los Angeles Country Club, a wooded forest surrounding a golf course. Max would scale the wall, where he could hide in the woods, and no one would witness the obscene transformation. He could rearrange himself in peace.

Max found the walls were just chain link fences, but much higher than he had anticipated. He was young and able. He found a spot where the vegetation was low enough to allow Max to hop over. He scaled the fence, swinging his leg over. Unfortunately, the fence itself was the city limit. As Max balanced up top, looking for a safe landing spot among the trees, he felt a familiar pain. The cursed cock grew so quickly that he lost balance and fell off the wall. The lights went out.

When Max came to, a trio of older golfers stood over him whispering. He blinked his eyes.

The closest golfer was a grey-haired man with a silly-looking golf outfit. He extended a hand and helped Max to his feet.

"Are you all right, son?"

Max nodded. He looked down and saw that his cock had grown in the worst possible way. It dangled out of the waist of his pants for all to see. The old man asked, "May I touch it?"

Max shrugged. "It doesn't have magical powers."

The trio of golfers laughed. They each took turns stroking and holding the giant cock. Despite himself, Max felt an erection stirring. He blushed. The men gasped as Max's cock began to swell even more.

The man with the silly outfit said, "Boy, you've been tricked by a shedim."

In answer to Max's puzzled expression, he said, "It's a tricky demon."

Max sighed. "I made a terrible bargain."

The oldest man said, "You need his name and who he serves. That will give you some power over him. Good luck." The three old men wandered off and vanished between the trees. Max hid behind a tree and began the arduous task of putting his gargantuan penis back inside his pants. He left the country club determined to get his life back.

SANTA MONICA

When the streetcar crossed Bundy Street, Max's penis shrank rapidly. It was still much bigger than anyone would want, but it was not like Chicago or Los Angeles. Santa Monica was its own little seaside town. Throughout the day, he felt his cock grow, thicken, and shrink. He realized it was because there were so many visitors to the boardwalk. They came and went, walking out of Santa Monica to Venice, an adjacent neighborhood of Los Angeles.

In some cases, the change was so noticeable that it caught the eye of passersby. One man said, "Hey buddy, gotta squirrel in your trousers?" He laughed and then promptly forgot why he was laughing.

Max had hoped to take a dip in the ocean, but with his cock's unpredictable fluctuations, he worried something obscene might occur. He found the wool trousers uncomfortable and longed to bathe in the cool ocean water in his Jantzen swimsuit. There were families with little children on the beach, so he kept walking North until the beach crowd changed. There was a drainage pipe that emptied into the ocean. Just the other side was an all-male beach. It figured the homosexuals would have to hide by toxic waste in order to have their own beach. But it was a lovely crowd. He saw some other men removing their pants and putting on trunks. They weren't ashamed of a little nudity. Max shrugged and pulled down his trousers. Every head on the beach turned and gasped. Max turned red.

Once his suit was on, and the unpredictable lunch meat in his shorts was wrapped around his hip, he ran into the January sea. It was colder than he expected. A few size queens still hadn't forgotten what they'd seen. They joined him in the water. One very pushy queen named Godwin approached him and put his hand on the monster just as it changed size. Godwin gasped.

"How did you do that?"

Max played dumb and shrugged.

"No, seriously, one minute it was long and thin, the next it was still soft but, but— "

Godwin had forgotten him. He swam further North to get away from the drain pipe. Suddenly, his penis shriveled into its old tiny size. There was a strip of beach that was unincorporated. If he went any further North, he'd be in the Palisades, which were part of Los Angeles. He decided to have fun with the crowd.

He came out of the water and made a line in the sand where Santa Monica began. He took off his swimsuit, giving the whole beach a glimpse of his tiny penis. When enough people were watching, he stepped forward, causing his cock to swell suddenly to great size. He could hear shrieks and moans coming from the queens on the beach. He walked, naked, to where he had left his pants. He stood watching the water for a while, letting the whole beach take in the enormity of his cock. It was satisfying, and for a brief moment, it felt worth the awful bargain he made with Barbax.

A single young man approached him. "Quite the show, Max."

"Do I know you?" Suddenly he was filled with dread. Think of the Devil, and he shall appear. "Oh. Hi, Barbax."

The young man's face morphed until it was the familiar green eyes with dark curly locks. "Who gets to be mommy this time?"

Max looked around. They were on a barren beach with hundreds of witnesses. "I don't think we can do anything here in the open."

The demon snapped his fingers, and a cottage sprung up around them, with white walls, white linen curtains, and a four-poster bed with a mattress made of goose down. Barbax pushed Max onto the bed. "I think you should be mommy today."

Max hated himself because he wanted it so badly. The demon put his serpentine cock into Max and made his insides quiver. Max thrashed about on the bed, unable to believe that sex could feel this good. Barbax was a talented fucker.

The sun set, and the demon was still inside Max, making him orgasm in his ass. Max's eyes rolled back as he thrashed about, overpowered by pleasure. He tried to kiss Barbax, who pushed his face into the bed.

Max looked like a child who was told he wouldn't have Christmas this year.

The demon laughed. "I'm gonna soak your guts with my demon seed." And he did. Max lay on the mattress, floating in self-loathing, eyes closed. When he opened them, he was lying on the beach naked, staring up into the face of a police officer.

"Come on, buddy. Jacking off on the beach is illegal."

Max put his pants on. The cop slapped cuffs on him. "You were out of your mind. I nearly radioed for a psych evaluation. Are you out of your mind?"

Max sighed. He just had to wait a few minutes, and he would be free. He dragged his feet as he walked to the cop car.

The cop was a blabbermouth. "Honestly, that's the

biggest fucking dick I've ever seen. And I've seen plenty."

It was a hint, but Max wasn't in the mood.

"Can you remind me what I'm being charged with?"

The cop stopped, puzzled. "Drunk and disorderly? No. Was it?"

"You pinched the wrong guy."

The cop nodded. "Yeah, yeah, I did. I'm awful sorry."

He undid the handcuffs. "Can I give you a ride somewhere?"

"Just to the bluffs. I can find my way home from there."

Before they even got to the bluffs, the cop turned around.

"Who the fuck are you?"

❈ 19 ❈

SEARCHING

Max was tired of his cock changing sizes every five minutes. He decided to walk to Venice Beach and admire the canals, even if it meant lugging around the albatross from hell. As soon as he crossed into Venice, he made a beeline for the changing rooms. Once his penis was thoroughly subdued, he went for a stroll on the boardwalk. He felt relieved knowing his cock would stay this size as long as he shared the city with the men responsible for its preposterous dimensions. The devil had mentioned someone, a blond aspiring actor with a cock that almost dragged on the ground. He must be responsible for the length. He doubted the man was also responsible for the impossible girth. But who knows? He tried to put it out of his mind, but it sat behind his eyes, like an itch in the brain. Everywhere he walked, he looked for someone with the same size problem as his. Los Angeles was an enormous city. How would he ever find his cock twin?

Max caught a streetcar back to his fleabag hotel downtown. He hadn't been there in a few days but had the key. He vowed to devote his days to tracking down his cock twin. His first stop was the Gower Gulch. That's where all the Western films were shot. Cowboys hung about hoping to get a small part but usually got hired as extras instead. If the blond behemoth were a cowboy, he would no doubt be hanging around the Gulch.

Max found his research easy. You could talk about penis size to anyone if they were going to forget the conversation. He approached one stoic cowboy who leaned against the window of the Columbus Drugstore.

The cowboy nodded in his direction.

"Excuse me, sir, is there a cowboy here with a mammoth penis?"

The cowboy frowned.

Max continued. "I mean, like one cowboy whose dick is beyond big. Our studio is looking for him. We heard about him."

The cowboy shook his head. "Ain't no one like that here."

A few more queries, and he determined the blond was not among the cowboys. He did see one cowboy with a long thick cock crawling toward his knee, but that wasn't his dick twin.

The next stop was Sunset and Crescent Heights at Schwab's drugstore. Actors with no phone always knew they could give a casting agent the pay phone at Schwab's. It was a code amongst the stars and starlets that they would take a message if the lucky one wasn't at the store. So it became the place to see and be seen. Directors, Producers, and Agents all made a point of stopping by Schwab's looking for raw talent on the cheap.

Max posed as a producer. "Excuse me, sir." A handsome blond turned to face him.

"Yeah?"

Max didn't mince words. "And we need it to be gargantuan. It's not illegal if it's covered up, you see."

The blond, whose name was Cliff, nodded.

"Couldn't you just put a salami in his pants or whatever?"

Max shook his head. "It's got to be the real thing."

Cliff tapped a young girl on the shoulder. "Betsy, this cat wants some guy with a huge, uh, you know. Ring any bells?"

Betsy said, "No. Let me ask Patsy." It didn't take long for the crowd at Schwab's to come up with a name.

Betsy came back. "You're looking for Long John Philips. It's a double entendre, get it?"

"Is he on a set?"

"Yeah, he booked a show at Warner Brothers on Santa Monica Boulevard near La Brea. I think it's called 'Made for the Maid' or something like that. Oh, and he goes by LJ."

❧ 20 ❧

LONG JOHN

It wasn't hard for a forgettable man to talk his way into a movie studio with tougher security than the Soviet Union. Once you were past the gate, everyone just assumed you belonged there. The Warner Brothers lot was packed. Every sound stage was in operation. The roads between stages were narrow, barely allowing a truck to pass. Max found a chalkboard, and sure enough, there was a production on Stage 7 called "Made for the Maiden."

The sound stage was locked. A lighted sign read "Production in Progress."

Max was going to have to wait. After an hour, the bell rang, and the big door opened. A producer-type lit a cigar and looked at Max. "Who are you?"

Max said, "I'm Long John's stunt double."

The producer said, "Stunt double? LJ doesn't have a stunt double. He's barely got a part."

Max didn't want to make any further impression, fearing he would be remembered longer. He walked past the producer and onto the sound stage. It took a minute for his eyes to adjust to the dim light. The set was dark for the moment. From what he could overhear, it was a lunch break. There was a table full of fresh fruit, soggy sandwiches, and day-old pastries. Max had a few grapes and a stale donut.

"Are you an extra?" A pretty girl with a kewpie doll face looked inquisitively at Max.

"No, I'm a stunt double."

The girl grabbed his hand. "Don't eat at the extras table! Come on." She dragged him to a back room where three giant tables overflowed with stuffed turkey, ham, cornbread, and food Max had never seen or heard of. Once the girl let go of his hand, she forgot him. He was glad not to have to make small talk.

It had been a long time since Max had been able to eat a full plate. He had found soup kitchens the best place for nourishment. Everybody there was invisible. He piled his plate high and sat in a canvas chair to enjoy the feast. That was when he spotted him.

Long John Philips had an otherworldly aura, like a halo around his blond hair. He walked with a slight limp that Max knew all too well. When he laughed, he revealed a perfect row of white teeth. Max stared unabashedly, as was his habit. It was one of the perks of being forgettable. He caught LJ's eye, and the blond Adonis limped to his chair.

"Hey, I haven't seen you before, have I?" LJ extended his hand. "Long John Philips."

"Max Andrews."

LJ said, "There's something about you, Max. I can't place my finger on it. I feel like we know each other."

Max shrugged and adjusted his cock in an obvious manner. "I'm your stunt double."

LJ laughed. "I play a butler. I don't do any stunts."

"Okay, I'm your dick twin." Max smiled. He could say anything because LJ would forget him in a minute.

"Impossible. Nobody is big enough to claim that," LJ said.

Through his pants, Max squeezed his cock head

that hung just above his ankle. LJ made a choking sound.

"Holy moly! You ain't kidding. Listen, I gotta take a leak. Do you?"

The two men stood side by side at a floor-length urinal trough. They both pulled and pulled to release the giant hiding in their pants.

Max looked to be the same length and girth, but he was a hair longer and a fraction thicker.

LJ put his arm around his twin. "I'll bet you scare off all the women."

Max shrugged. "I don't try with women. I find it best if I let men fuck me."

LJ nodded. "Yeah, I ain't never found a person that could take me. I certainly wouldn't want to fuck you."

The two men left the restroom and strolled around the Warner lot, exchanging tips and tricks. LJ had lived with it his whole life, so he knew much more than Max.

Any minute, Long John Philips would get that cloudy look in his eyes and wonder why he was standing with a stranger. But an hour passed, and they were still talking.

Max decided to tell LJ about his bargain. "In truth, I'm hung very, very small. So small, I can't fuck anyone."

LJ nodded. "Barbax. Fucking asshole."

Max grabbed his dick twin by the lapel. "You know him?"

LJ said, "I wouldn't be on this set if it weren't for him."

The two men felt something building between them. It was unfamiliar to Max. He felt more than a friendly feeling for the handsome blond boy. He might be the first man to remember him this long. Max dreaded each second that passed, afraid LJ's eyes would grow foggy and he would lose whatever was growing between them.

The bell rang, signaling that lunch was over.

LJ turned to Max, "You stay right there. I ain't done yet." He strolled back onto the set.

Max grew tearful. He feared that terrible moment when LJ would forget him.

At the end of the day, LJ sauntered over to Max.

Max fully expected an introduction and a handshake, but LJ said, "Let's continue over dinner."

Max smiled. "I'm buying."

LJ grinned. "Good, because we're going out for steak dinner."

⚬⚬⚬

THEY DECIDED TO MEET AT MUSSO AND FRANK, THE new steakhouse on Hollywood Boulevard. They agreed to wear more revealing clothing just to turn a few heads. LJ wasn't famous yet. He suggested the publicity stunt. Max wore tight khaki-colored trousers that accentuated his size rather than hiding it. He figured he would be stood up, but LJ was different. He broke all records for remembering him. Max stood outside the fancy restaurant on the Boulevard. His pants and their contents turned many heads.

Just when Max gave up hope, LJ came strolling down the street in tight white trousers that left nothing to the imagination. A minor car accident occurred, and a man walked into a traffic sign. He waved at Max, who breathed a sigh of relief.

They sat at a booth. Waiters and customers walked by, trying to be discreet as they peeked under the table.

LJ had a million questions. "What did you give up, and what did you ask for?"

Max said, "I promised him my soul and asked to have the biggest dick in town. I hadn't factored in the need to change towns from time to time."

LJ sucked air. "Oh. I can see how that plays out. I

promised my soul, too. In exchange, I get to be an actor. I forgot to include fame in the equation."

Max said, "Did he include any clauses?"

LJ said, "Isn't it obvious? He gave me the world's
biggest dick to carry around. I was big before, but now
I'm just, well, you know what it's like. At least you can
travel and change sizes. So, what's your clause?"

Max said, "I'm forgotten by everyone who knows
me or sees me. Nobody remembers me."

LJ cut into his filet. "I was stuck with another one,
too. I remember everyone I meet! It's worse than it
sounds. Imagine buying a hot dog, and the vendor never
leaves your memory. It starts to hurt."

Max took another spoonful of creamed spinach. "I
got stuck with a second one, too. If a man asks to fuck
me, I have to do it. I have no choice."

LJ said, "So if I asked you to let me fuck you, you'd
have to do it? That could kill you!"

Max agreed. "Please don't."

LJ said, "Don't worry, my friend, I'm only into guys
with little peckers."

Max underestimated how lonely he had been.
Having someone call him friend nearly brought tears to
his eyes. He wiped at the corners.

LJ put his fork down. "Is everything okay?"

Max said, "You're the only person who has remembered me since that awful day. I'm sorry. I didn't mean
to upset you."

LJ took Max's hand. "Don't fret. The demon didn't
plan for us to meet. I mean, I break one of your clauses.
I'll bet we could outsmart him."

❧ 21 ❧

TIP YOUR WAITER

Max hadn't thought about it in a while. There must be a way out of the contract. The waiter approached the table. "More bread?"

LJ waved him away, but he stood there, smiling. It was Barbax.

Max pounded the table, making the silverware jump. "Get the fuck out!" It came out in a harsh whisper.

Barbax said, "Whoa, whoa. I'm not here to fuck with you. I just want to check in and see how it's going. Maybe we can bargain further."

LJ said, "I've had enough of your bargaining. I don't know why you gave me this huge cock, but it was a dirty trick."

Barbax shrugged. "You'll figure it out." He turned to Max. "And how is your wish working out?"

Max didn't want to give Barbax the pleasure of a response, but he couldn't help himself. "You made everybody forget me. What good is it to be the biggest if no one remembers?"

Barbax winked. "You're getting it. Your friend is slow."

LJ growled. "Listen, it don't make no sense. None at all."

Barbax shrugged. "Let me help you connect the dots. How many leading roles have you auditioned for?"

LJ said, "Dozens."

Barbax said, "And yet you always get handed a minor role. Why do you think that is?"

LJ said, "Part of your curse."

The devilish waiter chuckled. "In a way. I don't really influence anyone. It's you."

LJ shook his head. "I don't follow you, man."

Barbax sighed. "You are so dense. Okay, let me make it plain. There's no hiding your cock from a casting director. They want you in the film, but they can't risk you being in the foreground. Your reputation precedes you. Everyone who matters knows you're hung like a horse and hippopotamus."

Before LJ could say another word, the waiter vanished.

A FRIENDSHIP LIKE NO OTHER

Max paid the bill. The two men walked to LJ's apartment nearby. He had a sofa with Max's name on it.

LJ had to be on set at dawn. When Max woke up, LJ was already gone. The apartment was a mess. Max was bored, so he cleaned the place. It felt good to do the dishes for someone who might remember him. After Barbax saw him so obviously happy, he feared he would make LJ forget. But when he got home, LJ remembered. He even brought barbecue sandwiches from the stand up the street.

LJ was grateful for the clean apartment. "You can stay here as long as you like. I wouldn't want you to be out among the people who forget you with no place to return."

Max was touched. He felt that unusual stirring in his heart. LJ was blunt. "I gotta confess, I don't like wearing trousers, so I usually walk around my place naked. Will that bother you?"

Max shook his head. "Go ahead."

LJ said, "Hey, Max, why don't you take off your clothes, too? It feels really good."

The two men shucked their clothing, enjoying the breeze on their humongous cocks while they munched on barbecue sandwiches. They exchanged tips for managing their curses.

Max said, "I got a pair of custom-made trousers with elastic bands. It hides everything."

LJ said, "I think it's too late. Everyone knows. I wonder if I can escape the curse if I agree not to be an actor."

Max shook his head. "I doubt it. Next time we see him, we can ask."

The blond man said, "How did you even find me?"

Max said, "Barbax told me to go find you."

LJ's face turned the color of Easter lilies. "Oh shit, that can't be good. He's up to something."

Max admired his new friend. His muscular chest was covered with downy blond hair. His biceps flexed every time he moved his hands. LJ caught him staring.

"You like what you see?"

Max nodded. "You're very handsome."

"You're a looker, too. If I wasn't into women, and we didn't both have these useless dicks, I'd fuck you."

It came dangerously close to an expressed desire for sex. Max felt a mild compulsion to give his ass to Long John. It passed.

"Careful, you almost triggered a curse."

LJ laughed hard. "I said 'if.' I'll be careful. I don't want to go to jail for murder by dick."

Max was surprised by his disappointment. He couldn't possibly take LJ up his ass, and yet he wanted to feel connected to this man who didn't forget him.

A few weeks passed like this. Max left the apartment during the day to shoplift a few items and pay for others. Each night when LJ got home, they took off their clothes and ate whatever he brought home for dinner.

One night LJ said, "Why do you wait for me to get home to take off your clothes? I don't mind if you're naked when I get here."

Max said, "I guess I like getting naked together."

LJ tilted his head. "If I didn't know better, I'd say you were a little queer for me."

Max shrugged. "Aren't you a little queer for me?"

LJ shook his head. "I thought about it. I can't stand seeing that big dick. If you were hung small, it would be a different story. Your ass is big, the way I like, but that dick is a wet blanket."

Max knew he would probably die if he ever let LJ fuck him, but he wanted to go out with a bang. He said, "Put your clothes on. We're going to the County Strip."

"On Sunset?"

"Yeah. You're gonna rent a room at the Chateau Marmont tonight. I want you to see something."

❧ 23 ❧

MARMONT REVISITED

A short streetcar ride brought Max over the city line. It hurt so bad that he doubled over, but his cock returned to its original size. He kept quiet to surprise his friend.

In the room, with a view of the ocean in the distance, LJ disrobed. Max delayed a little, maximizing the surprise factor. He let his trousers drop.

LJ said, "Fuck. How did you do that? I thought we'd be the same size wherever we went."

Max said, "This isn't a town." He lay on the bed, extending his arms. LJ joined his embrace, his already huge cock growing.

"Damn. That's the perfect dick. I like to blow little guys." He kneeled on the floor, his head between Max's legs, licking and sucking on the tiny penis. Max let out a loud sigh. LJ was a good friend. He put his tongue up Max's asshole. Max wriggled under the tickling tongue.

LJ buried his face in Max's bulbous butt cheeks. He hummed and licked, making Max squirm with delight. He lifted his head and said, "God damn, I wanna fuck you!"

Max would get his wish, fucked to death by the only man who remembers him. The powerful cords of the curse flipped him onto his stomach, his ass in the air.

LJ tried to resist. "Oh shit. Oh no. I'm sorry, man."

Max had brought a tub of Vaseline in his bag for this occasion. He handed it to LJ, who quickly placed a portion on Max's ass and used a lot more to get himself greased up.

LJ was unable to prevent the curse from happening. He brought his cock to the hole and pushed.

Max felt a ripping sensation as LJ plowed into him. There was no holding back. The urgency of the curse took away all gentleness. LJ's massive cock stretched Max further than he thought possible. His ass was on fire. The thick head invaded his innards, pushing forward in ever more painful thrusts. At last, LJ's hips rested on Max's behind. "I'm so sorry, buddy."

Max said, "It's okay. It's what I wanted."

It was impossible to know if LJ was a gentle lover. The curse took away all softness. The powerful fucking was brutal. Max bled on the huge cock, making LJ even more upset.

"Oh god, I don't want you to die!"

Max said, "Keep going; I can take it." He was lying but didn't want LJ to be upset or guilty when he killed him.

LJ pounded and pounded. "Since it got this big, it takes forever to cum."

Max rotated to face his invader. He pinched LJ's nipples. LJ trembled, momentarily losing momentum. Then the hard fucking continued.

Max said, "If you kiss me, I'm sure it will help."

LJ didn't wait. He planted his lips on Max's, one man's lips exploring the other's, tongues intertwined. The kiss made Max's little dick stand up. LJ rubbed it with his hand.

Then a miracle happened. Max's pain subsided, only to be replaced with intense spasms of pleasure. It was happening. The kiss had sent him into a full-body orgasm. His muscles tightened and loosened, squeezing

LJ's monstrous cock in rhythm to his violent thrusts. Max returned his focus to LJ's nipples.

"Oh god, that feels so good. Max, are you dying?"

Max shook his head. "I think I'm going to survive this."

LJ planted his lips on Max's. They kissed with renewed fervor, fueling the twitching and jerking that rippled through Max's body.

Max pulled away. "LJ, I'm gonna come."

LJ stopped rubbing him. "I'm close. Hang on."

He lifted Max's head to his nipple. Max latched on, sucking, nibbling, and biting.

"Oh shit, Max, you're so fucking sexy. Keep doing that. Just like that."

Max obeyed. His insides, stretched to their limits, were quivering against LJ's manhood. That must have been enough because LJ lifted his head and said, "Oh god, Oh god." He rubbed Max until the orgasm was unavoidable. Max shot cum onto his friend's pubic bush, belly, and chest.

"Aaaargh!" LJ unloaded a considerable volume of cum in his friend. He collapsed, exhausted from the compulsive fucking. Max's eyes fluttered. He had lost a little blood, but he survived.

LJ brought him around with a kiss. He said, "Next time, I won't say it out loud."

Max didn't know if he could take a next time. He ran for the bathroom to wipe up the blood. It was bright red, which meant it wasn't serious. In a minute or two, it stopped.

LJ was standing at the bathroom door, startling Max when he opened it. The sheets looked like a small animal had been sacrificed.

"Are you sure you're okay?"

Max nodded. Each step he took was a new level of pain. He was so stretched out that he could feel wind blowing up his butt. "If I die, I'll die happy." Then he fainted.

Max came to with a private doctor crouched over him. LJ was struggling to make the doctor finish his work.

"You're having memory problems, man. You said the patient needed a stitch.

Max said, "Am I still bleeding?"

LJ breathed a sigh of relief. "You're awake. I was so fucking worried."

The doctor closed his case. "I don't remember saying he needed a stitch. I checked, and he's healing. No anal sex for a week."

Max said, "I can wait. Can you?"

FRIENDS TO LOVERS

A week later, Max was walking right and could close his asshole. He was curious to know if the next time would be any better. It was too much for Max, but LJ wanted it. As long as he took it slowly, Max would be able to take it. He thought a cock as big as Max's would be more satisfying than regular big dicks. It wasn't. LJ admitted that he wished he were normal. Sex with such a big cock was difficult, time-consuming, and dangerous.

Max was feeling a growing, intense desire to be around LJ. On the days when his friend was on set, Max felt lonely.

One night he asked, "Do you miss me?"

LJ put down his burger. "You mean now?"

Max said, "No, I mean when you're on set. Do you miss me?"

LJ nodded. "It's painful how much I miss you."

Max glowed. "Is it possible that this is love?"

LJ said, "I ain't never been in love, but if this is what it feels like, it's better than I could have imagined."

Max was ready to try again. He handed Max a tub of Vaseline and put his finger to his lips. "You don't mind if I'm big, do you?"

LJ said, "I can work with it."

The logistics of being fucked with a third leg were tricky. Max kneeled on the sofa, placing the monstrous cock in front of his chest. He leaned against it, offering his ass to his friend.

LJ licked Max's ass with great enthusiasm. His tongue relaxed his hole. LJ coated his hand in Vaseline and slowly, carefully lubricated his friend. The hole was so relaxed that his entire hand went inside. Max couldn't believe how gentle LJ could be when not compelled by a curse.

With the same care, he pushed his lubricated cock into Max. In a smooth, gentle motion, he pushed until he met resistance. Max touched LJ's knee to slow him, but he was already pulling back slowly, preparing for a second push forward. He continued this way, in sharp contrast to his brutal impaling at the Marmont. Max shivered with desire. LJ was going so slowly, Max actually reached behind him and pulled him closer, the big cock finishing the long journey up his entrails.

Max said, "Baby, you're so good at this."

LJ chuckled. "I was pretty damn big before this. I got the technique as long as it ain't your curse."

Instead of long, vicious strokes, LJ pushed and pulled in short strokes, keeping himself buried inside Max. As he moved back and forth, his cock swelled, stretching his friend's insides.

Max was close to another body orgasm. LJ was slowly increasing the length and strength of his strokes, which only grew more intense as he swelled to his maximum hardness.

"Oh, Jesus." Max breathed hard. "Oh Jesus, here it comes."

His insides began to push against LJ with a rhythmic pulse. Max's back curled like a scared cat, then bowed like a milk cow. The pulse became spasms. Max nearly cried with joy. He needed this man inside him.

LJ clasped his hands behind his head and humped Max with more intensity. "Shit, that feels good."

Max's internal twitching prevented him from speaking in words. "Oh. Oh. Uh. Oh."

LJ grabbed Max's hips and banged into him hard and fast. He put one hand on the small of Max's back and changed his rhythm to long, undulating waves of fucking. Then he changed again to the violent thrusts he had used the first time.

Max could barely stand the brutal fucking. He refrained from saying anything but was sure he was wounded again. Soon, he didn't have to say anything when LJ saw the blood on his cock.

"Oh God, Max, I'm hurting you. I'm so sorry."

Max said, "It doesn't hurt. Keep going." It was true. The nerves in his innards were few and far between.

Minutes passed, with LJ pounding away at his friend. Max sucked air between his teeth to mitigate the painful onslaught. LJ knew how to warm a guy up, but he didn't know how to fuck with a man-killing cock. It was time for Max to say something.

"Oh, god, that's too good. I love it when you go slow."

LJ obeyed. It was more of the gentle fucking. He ran his fingers through Max's hair, held it in his hands, and pulled his head back for a kiss. The kiss was the tipping point. LJ took extremely long strokes, nearly popping his head out and quickly snaking his way inside. Max was surprised to see his own huge cock grow hard. He rubbed the head with his palm. After his body orgasm, it didn't take long until he was close. LJ saw the colossal cock and turned away. He said he liked Max's real penis, the one that resembled a cashew.

Max never knew love, but he was pretty sure this was it. He had already used the L word in other contexts. Should he use it now? He couldn't think; he was shivering with pleasure.

LJ said, "I can't take much more of you twitching all up in there. Damn, you're gonna make me cum!"

Max said, "I'm almost there, too." He continued to rub the head of his giant cock. It started to leak on his palm, leaving long, sticky threads of clear fluid stuck to his hand. He used it to rub even faster.

LJ picked up the pace again, unable to stop or slow the inevitable climax because of Max's churning insides. "Here I come."

Max said, "Yeah, come, baby, come. I'm right behind you."

LJ opened the floodgates and filled Max with his warm cum. Max said, "Now. It's now. Now." And he drained his balls dry with a hot shower of cum that covered them both.

Smoking cigarettes, they talked about sex. LJ said, "I dig fucking you. I wish you could be small all the time."

"We could move to the Strip."

LJ laughed. There were no houses along that long stretch of sin and corruption. He said, "You sure you want to take all of this?"

He gestured to his softening cock.

Max paused. He didn't want to tell the truth that it was tearing him apart. It would upset LJ. "When you fuck me, it's like nothing matters."

LJ said, "I used to like women, but you turned me. That ass of yours is so pretty; I wanna fuck it all the time."

He triggered the curse.

Exhausted from the previous session, Max was forced to raise his ass in the air. LJ stuffed the gaping hole with his rapidly hardening cock. Max didn't let LJ see him cry as the poor man involuntarily fucked Max half to death.

Max turned to face LJ, so he could tease his nipples. LJ made a face and pushed Max's gargantuan cock out of the way. Max twisted his nipples, and LJ kissed him. Those two things, the kiss and the nipples, made it easier for LJ to come. His brutal thrusts were injuring Max, who cried out in pain. LJ tried to pull out, but the curse wouldn't let him. He pounded and pounded, unable to resist the terrible spell.

Max lay on his back, feeling weak from the vicious fucking and blood loss. "Don't worry, baby. I'm fine. I'm fine."

LJ said, "I don't want to hurt you. You know that, right?"

Max lied. "It doesn't hurt. Keep going." Max's cock remained soft. The pain was interfering with his pleasure circuits. He lifted his head and sucked on LJ's nipple. That seemed to help. LJ's pace quickened, causing more damage but bringing him closer to climax. "I'm almost there, little buddy. I'm so sorry."

Max was delirious. He said, "Take your time. I love you."

LJ said, "Holy shit. I love you, too!" They kissed passionately. At last, LJ stopped, buried all the way inside his love, releasing a second load to join the first that was still deep in Max's guts.

Max felt the cum mingle with his torn insides. When LJ pulled out, a red and white river flowed, eventually turning completely red. Max was close to fainting. He tried to stand up to get a tissue, but once on his legs, he stumbled and passed out.

✣ 25 ✣

TERRIBLE BEDSIDE MANNER

Max awoke in the hospital. LJ hovered, squeezing his hat.

"Max? Are you awake?"

Max nodded weakly. "What happened?"

LJ blushed. "I had to take you to the hospital. They said you'd be dead if it had been five minutes more."

The doctor pulled back the curtain. "How's our patient? Max, is it?"

"How did you know?"

"I read your chart." The doctor played with his lapel.

"How long have I been here?" Max's eyes narrowed.

"I'd say eighteen hours, more or less."

Max spit out his next words. "Fuck you, Barbax."

The doctor laughed and pulled off his cap, revealing a head of curly black hair. He took off his face mask, revealing his beard. He turned to Max. "I know you're starting to get it. But are you, LJ?" He turned his head quizzically toward the handsome blond actor.

LJ said, "Get what?"

Barbax laughed. "You simple-minded fool. I asked for your souls in return for these gifts. How do you think I collect?"

Max answered him. "You give us everything we wanted but add clauses that make the gifts useless."

Barbax smiled. "Yes, that's part of it. Where does your soul reside?"

LJ said, "In the heart." A look of horror washed over his face.

Barbax said, "Correct! I leave it to you to figure out what I've done. And when you have, I'll be watching your faces." And he left the hospital room.

LJ was crying. He must have understood something Max hadn't. "It ain't right. It ain't right."

Max lifted a hand weakly, and LJ took it. "What isn't right, my love?"

LJ said, "Our love. It will destroy us."

And suddenly, Max understood. Barbax wanted them to meet because they were doomed to fall in love. It was even more twisted than he had imagined. The love was deadly. LJ was the only person in the world who knew who he was. And Max loved him. And it would kill him.

Even if LJ somehow managed to get his curse lifted, he would forget who Max was. And if Max had his curse lifted, LJ would remember him. But LJ was too big to be with anyone, so their love would never include sex. LJ deserved to find love. Max vowed that if it were a choice, LJ should be the one to have the curse lifted. He kept it to himself.

Then something about what the old golfers said to him came to the surface. If they could find out who he serves, it would weaken him. And if he could find a hole in the contract, he could get out of it. He knew what they needed to do.

26

PALMISTRY

Max wasn't discharged; he was simply forgotten. LJ helped him put on his clothes. "Where are we?"

LJ said, "Near Echo Park. The Queen of Angels Hospital."

Max said, "Let's catch a streetcar."

The streetcar dropped them near the hotel that Max had long since vacated. Just up Fourth Street was the palm reader he had seen on his way to the tailor.

The two men entered the shop, which smelled of incense and cigars. A beautiful woman with soft eyes and delicate hands greeted them. "Oh, this isn't good. This isn't good. Come, sit. Hold his hand, or I'll forget."

Max was impressed. This lady knew the mysteries of the occult.

"I cannot lift a curse from your head. I simply cannot because you brought it upon yourselves."

Max nodded. "I know. We want to know something that we believe you can tell us."

"The demon he serves?"

Max wondered how this woman could suck knowledge out of his head. For a brief instant, he feared she was Barbax. But she was just a really intuitive reader.

"Tell me his name. I have a book. It may take a

while." She gathered a pen and paper, but she wasn't quick enough.

Max said, "His name is Barbax."

She shook her head. "It's terrible luck to hear the name of a demon and even worse to speak it. Be careful."

Max said, "I'm sorry."

She waved her hand in the air. "I help you. It's okay."

She pulled down a large volume called "The Lesser Key of Solomon."

She flipped through it silently. "Ah!" Her finger landed on a page with a blood stain. "I find it. Here, let me write. Do not say out loud."

Using a carpenter's pencil, she wrote down two names.

Max took the paper and looked at it. "Why two?"

She said, "He is servitor of both these Arch-Demons. One demon he favors men...yes, men like yourselves who have sex with other men. He protects them." She put her finger on the name Asmodeus.

"The other one is creator of lust and vanity. He used to be woman, but he became man, almost like you." She pointed to Max's crotch, then put her finger on the name Ashtaroth.

"I warn you; your little imp will be angry if you say their names. Be careful. He has already tricked you."

LJ hadn't said a word the entire time. He leaned forward and said, "I was raised to worship Jesus Christ. This is not my scene, no, ma'am."

She said, "Good. Oh good. You will have Christ with you. Take this." She gave LJ a bronze crucifix. "Don't use it unless you have no choice."

The two lovers returned to LJ's apartment.

Max hoped they could get out from under their respective curses and live life like ordinary men again. LJ would end up killing Max with his cock. Max would be

doomed to walk the earth with an ever-changing humongous cock. He didn't want a big cock anymore. He
wanted LJ, and LJ preferred Max with his extremely
small penis.

LJ looked at his partner. "You've been quiet an awful
long time. What's happening in your head, Max?"

Max smiled. "I'm figuring out how to undo this
curse. If you look at it, our curses are intertwined into
one awful curse."

LJ said, "Star-crossed lovers."

Max said, "Demon-crossed lovers."

LJ cooked supper so Max could convalesce. He
made roasted chicken with spoon-bread and collard
greens. Max liked the little bits of bacon in the greens.

LJ pointed to the water at the bottom of the pot.
"Drink the pot liquor. It's got healing properties."

Max drank the wonderful brew. It made him feel
alive. They went to Van de Kamp's on Vine for coffee
and bear claws. They walked home arm in arm, turning
the heads of the crotch-watchers. Max was going to
miss being big.

27

DOOR TO DOOR SALESMAN

LJ had a 5:30 call. Max groaned as he bent to pick up the sweepings on the kitchen floor. He was banged up inside. He reached back and felt his hole, marveling at how loose it was. His fingers came back with a few spots of blood. He decided to stop cleaning and lie down. He closed his eyes and had just drifted off to sleep when a knock came at the door.

It was a Hoover vacuum salesman. Max wasn't prepared, and the man invited himself in. He prattled on about the amazing machine that would revolutionize house cleaning as we know it.

"See this beauty; she's built as solid as Fort Knox. Not a single speck of dust escapes because of the proprietary filter."

Max's mind shut down, and the sales pitch became a jagged series of noises and notes.

"How much do you think you would pay for a beautiful vacuum cleaner like this?"

Max came out of his reverie.

"I don't know. Seven dollars?"

The salesman laughed. "For seven dollars, I'll sell you the hose. This is a fine-tuned machine."

Max was irritated. The salesman kept on with his incessant pitch.

He said, "Say, Max, how much would you pay if this vacuum cleaner could suck up a curse? Get you out of your obligations to a certain demon?"

Max groaned. "Fuck you, Barbax."

Barbax said, "I would very much like to fuck you, sir."

Max had no choice but to let the man fuck him with his long, serpentine cock. After LJ, Barbax's cock felt like a vacation. Barbax had contended he was the best fuck, and he wasn't wrong. Max felt shivers of pleasure despite himself. He was disgusted with his own wanton lack of control. Barbax's slithering cock had healing properties. Max could feel his wounds and bruises healing at the touch of his penis. It intensified the shivers. Max's colossal penis dribbled clear drops that Barbax licked up like an ice cream cone. The demon was quick. In five minutes, he grunted and spilled his seed. Max held back; he didn't want to give Barbax the satisfaction of seeing him come.

Barbax said, "You didn't climax. I want you to fuck me."

Max was compelled to fuck the demon. He tried to take out his frustrations with violent thrusts, but they only served to make the demon moan with pleasure.

"Harder, Max. I can take it."

Max felt nauseated seeing his impossibly large cock disappear into the loose ass. He had pictured the lips around the entrance as a mouth; now, he couldn't get the image of being eaten out of his mind. He couldn't hurt the demon, no matter how hard he tried. He gave up and gave in to pleasure. Just as he reached climax, LJ walked in.

❧ 28 ❧

RUMPELSTILTSKIN

Max pulled out, bringing a river of cum that was too much just to be his. The demon had other men in his thrall. Max hurriedly stuffed his cock into his jeans as if he could somehow fool LJ into believing the demon and he were merely having a cup of tea together.

LJ said, "Don't worry, Max. I know it ain't your fault."

The demon turned to LJ. "Care to fuck me?"

LJ said, "No, thanks." He wasn't compelled like Max.

Barbax folded his arms and sat on the sofa. "I don't know if you get what it means to promise me your soul. I'm not going to snatch your spirit at death. No, giving me your soul means intense suffering while you're alive. I'm pretty close, right?"

Nobody spoke. Max looked at LJ, who looked at the floor.

The demon continued. "The worst suffering is heartache. I brought you together, and now my plan is unfolding. You are madly in love, but LJ will likely kill Max the next time he expresses his desire to fuck him. I'm particularly proud of that clause."

Max said, "Did Ashtaroth and Asmodeus sing your praises?"

The demon blanched. "H-how do you know their names?"

Max said, "Ashtaroth? Asmodeus? Come on. Everybody knows you serve them."

The demon said, "Please stop saying their names. You'll get me in trouble."

Max said, "So you aren't an all-powerful being after all. You have to answer to Ashtaroth and Asmodeus."

This infuriated Barbax. "You don't want to summon either one. I strongly suggest you cease to say their names at once."

Max said, "I'm already damned and doomed. What could they do that was any worse? I think you're afraid of what they can do to you."

LJ took out his crucifix. "Get thee behind me, Satan!"

Max continued. "So, if you don't want to get in trouble with your two bosses, I suggest we revisit our bargains."

Barbax stomped his foot. "Okay, I'll tell you what. I can remove the clauses from one of your contracts. I can't revoke the primary contract."

Max said, "Remove LJ's clauses. He'll have a career, his regular dick, and, unfortunately, he won't remember me. I will be heartbroken. So, you still get one soul."

LJ shook his head. "No, Max, I don't want to lose you. Take away your clauses." It was a rehearsed line.

Max said, "No, LJ, even if I was free from the clauses, you would still be too big, and I would, too."

LJ said, "We could move to the country. Out of town."

Max said, "Your acting career can hardly take off in Idaho."

LJ called on his acting skills. Tears welled up in his eyes. "But I can't lose you! Even if I completely forget you, I'll never fill up the hole in my heart. He'll still get my soul."

Barbax snickered. "So, what's it gonna be, boys? Max or LJ?"

Max gave LJ a pleading look, another bit of good acting. LJ relented. "Okay, you can lift my clauses in exchange for us never using your bosses' names again under one condition."

Barbax said, "I don't do conditions."

Max said, "Do Asmodeus and Astaroth know you don't do conditions?"

There was a roar from beneath the ground. They had awoken one of the Arch-Demons.

Barbax shook with fear. "You assholes woke up Asmodeus. Okay, okay, what's the condition?"

LJ said, "You gotta listen to Max for three minutes without interrupting. You gotta answer his questions truthfully."

Barbax laughed. "Got something to get off your chest, Max?"

Max nodded. "I've been meaning to say it for a while. You have to listen, and then you have to withdraw LJ's clauses."

Another roar from below the floorboards scared everyone.

Max said, "Do we have a bargain?"

Barbax hesitated. "I make the bargains."

Max said, "I'll just tell— "

Barbax said, "No! Don't say his name. You don't want to see what happens."

Max smiled. "Okay, listen to me. Let me start with a question. Where did we meet?"

Barbax said, "In my woods."

Max said, "When I introduced myself, who was I?"

Barbax frowned. "You were you."

Max said, "No. You said I was a brand-new person."

Barbax said, "You were Rowan Mallory."

Max leaned in close. "And who did you make your contract with?"

Barbax tried to run, but his own powers kept him rooted to the spot.

Max repeated his question.

Barbax answered truthfully. "I made a contract with Rowan Mallory."

"Did you make a contract with Max Andrews?"

Barbax grinned. "No, but I did add a clause on the airplane. You have to fuck any guy who says they want to."

Max asked, "Is a clause still valid if a contract is invalid?"

Barbax bit his tongue, trying not to answer. "Yes. Yes."

Max said, "So you've agreed to remove the clauses from LJ's contract, and you agree that my contract is invalid because it was made with a different person."

Barbax said, "No! NO! I don't agree!" A giant clawed hand broke through the floorboards and grabbed Barbax by his big balls, squeezing them.

Max said, "You have to tell the truth."

Barbax said, "Yes, yes. I agree." The hand let go.

Max said, "Say it. Say what you agree to."

Barbax said, "I agree to lift the clauses from LJ's contract, and I agree that your contract is invalid."

Max said, "No, you agree my contract is invalid, and then you will lift the contract." He knew LJ would forget him if it went in the other order.

The air crackled with electricity. Max felt his gargantuan penis shrink back down to its tiny size.

LJ, who wasn't used to changing sizes, doubled over in pain as his dick shrank from obscenely huge to very big.

Max looked Barbax in the eyes and saw fires burning inside. "You, sir, are forbidden from ever making a contract with me or LJ again."

Like Rumpelstiltskin, Barbax gnashed his teeth, stomped his feet, and threw a tantrum. The giant clawed hand grabbed him around the waist, pulling him down through the floorboards. The Arch-Demon laughed as he dragged his servitor down to the depths of Hell.

EPILOGUE

Max ran to LJ, who held him in a loving embrace.

LJ said, "Thank God it's all over."

Max sighed, twirling his fingers through LJ's exposed chest hairs. "I doubt God had much to do with it."

LJ said, "Do you think he'll be back?"

Max nodded. "I'm sure he'll try to fool us again. I'll tell him to get out in the name of Asmodeus."

LJ shivered. "Don't say that name!"

They laughed and curled up together on the couch, listening to the latest installment of The Shadow.

LJ put his hand on Max's knee and slowly moved to the crotch. Max was dying to know what LJ looked like down there. He shucked his dungarees and took off his shirt. LJ followed suit.

Under the baggy trousers was a genuinely spectacular cock. Soft, it hung halfway down his thigh. When he got hard, it almost reached his knee and swelled to a very nice girth.

When he put it inside Max, they both heard bells. They were perfect for each other. Max had been stretched beyond the limits of comprehension, but he was young and elastic. The sex was the best Max ever had, better than with Barbax and his snake dick.

LJ's contract had not been revoked, so he auditioned and got better and better roles. Now that his cock wasn't a handicap, the agents forgot about the man with the elephant trunk in his pants and saw "star" written all over his face.

They lived together as a gay couple. Hollywood turned a blind eye to LJ's lover. He wasn't quite famous enough to warrant a mention in Louella Parson's column, anyway.

It wasn't long before LJ got a few starring roles. They moved out of the apartment and bought a house in Beachwood Canyon. They lived there the rest of their lives.

BOOK TWO – DEMONIZED: STRAIGHT TO SISSY

by Adam Maxwell Bigglesworth

SATAN'S LITTLE SISSY

Paul Harris had a small problem. He was handsome, almost to the point of being a pretty boy, but his genitals were abnormally small. He didn't really care about his penis, but most women did. He was a little sensitive and shy. He faced constant rejection by women who wanted to be penetrated. He was too small to put in more than the very tip. He tried every position, but anatomy prevented him from going any further. He met a few women who liked having their pussies eaten out. He got very good at that but couldn't stand the taste. He just wanted to be with a woman who loved him as he was. He thought he'd explored the limits of sexuality and come up wanting. He was wrong.

One day, while walking along the shores of Lake Superior, he was greeted by an oddly-dressed man in a tailcoat and top hat. The man wore a hypnotic grin as he extended his hand. "I'm Hamaliel, but you can call me Ham."

Paul shook the man's hand. "That's an odd name. Where does it come from?"

Ham grinned even wider. "It's a Hebrew name, though I hail from Mesopotamia, originally."

Paul asked, "Is that like Iraq?"

The stranger nodded. He took Paul by the hand.

Paul was surprised when he shivered at the touch. It was pleasant.

Ham said, "I know you're discontent. I see it in your eyes. What is the matter, son?"

Paul sighed. "I want a woman who understands me. I want a woman who will let me have sex." He was surprised at how easily he could unburden himself with this perfect stranger.

Ham asked, "Are you dissatisfied with your size?"

Paul shook his head. "I can't change it, so I want to learn how to have sex in a way that it doesn't matter."

Ham ran a hand down Paul's back, sending spasms of pleasure along his spine. This was weird, and Paul knew it. But he didn't mind. The pleasant sensations were worth the strange fondling from this bizarre man.

Ham looked Paul in the eye. "If I told you I could give you what you want, would you wish for it?"

Paul nodded. "Yeah, I think I would like that."

Ham waved his hand and produced a lengthy document scrawled in cursive writing, making it very hard to read. "Sign here, and you can have your wish."

Paul pushed away. "That's a bunch of nonsense, and you know it."

Ham stroked Paul's hair, sending more shivers across his body. "You know it's true, boy. You have had disappointing sex for such a long time. Don't you want to know pleasure with a woman?"

Paul blushed. "Well, yeah."

Ham said, "Sign here. What do you have to lose?" He pressed an inked feather into Paul's hand.

"Fuck it." Paul signed the paper.

❧

Suddenly, the lake and woods disappeared. He was in a stone cell with no windows, completely naked. A single light bulb hung from the ceiling. He instinctively covered his tiny penis, a habit he'd had since his first shower in middle school. A clothes rack stood in the corner, and a plush, frilly canopy bed sat on the opposite wall. Ham came up behind Paul and squeezed his soft bottom.

"Oh, Paul, it's so soft. Like a woman's bottom, and shaped like it, too."

Paul wanted to protest, but the strokes from Ham's hand were intoxicating.

"You said you wanted to be with a woman who understands you, right?"

Paul nodded.

"Then who better understands you than yourself?"

Paul frowned. "I don't follow."

Ham chuckled. "You will soon, my boy. Now, cover that little penis. Go pick out some clothes."

Paul obeyed. He was dismayed that only women's garments hung from the rack. They were frilly, lacy underwear like you might find at Victoria's Secret or Frederick's of Hollywood. There were long, knee-high stockings and skimpy thongs. Spiky, shiny black high heels sat on the floor. The only actual choice for Paul was which color he wanted to wear.

"I don't see any pants. These are for women."

Ham's face curled into a snarl. "They're for you, little boy. Are you being ungrateful?"

Paul said, "No."

Ham said, "You will address me as 'Daddy' or 'Sir.'"

"No, sir."

Ham smiled. "You're learning quickly. I promise your wish will come true if you follow my every command. Put on some fucking clothes."

"Yes, sir."

Paul fumbled with the clothing, having never worn anything like it. He picked out flesh-colored stockings and a red thong. He put on the thong first, anxious to cover up his tiny penis. He had to sit on the floor to get the stockings on. As he stretched out his leg, he admired how they covered his leg hair and sparkled in the light of the bare bulb.

Ham said, "You like wearing women's clothes, don't you?"

Paul nodded.

Ham's smile faded. "I can't hear you."

"Yes. Yes, sir. I like it."

"You'll come to love it, I promise."

Paul stood, adjusting the thong so the skinny fabric string rested between his butt cheeks. He stepped into the high heels. He felt extremely awkward. He could barely walk in the heels. A full-length mirror appeared. Paul turned, surprised at how feminine his butt looked in that underwear. He'd never really noticed how plump it was.

Ham put a firm hand at the base of Paul's spine. "You want to put on makeup and a wig, right?"

"Yes, sir. I do, sir." Paul had never felt so free before. He was not pursuing a woman; he was becoming one. A makeup table appeared, and Paul sat down. A long, blond wig sat on a mannequin head. He studied the mannequin's painted makeup and did his best to imitate it.

Ham watched. "Not so much eye shadow. Take it off and try again."

Paul used the moist towelettes to remove the eye makeup. He'd gotten the lipstick just right. Ham grunted his approval.

"Thank you, Daddy."

After years of trying to be the man, Paul felt tremendous relief to take the female role. His little penis grew hard and began to dribble in the crotch of the thong.

"Your pussy's getting wet, isn't it, little girl?"

Paul nodded, hoping it wasn't a bad thing. Ham put

a firm hand on the wet spot, getting a little droplet on his finger. He tasted it.

"Your pussy juice tastes good, little girl."

"Thank you, Daddy." Paul smiled as he put on the wig.

Ham picked up Paul, his arm muscles bulging through his suit sleeves. He laid Paul on his back atop the canopy bed.

Ham slowly unbuttoned his tuxedo pants. Paul was intrigued, then terrified, as Ham pulled out a colossal cock, easily twenty times bigger than his own tiny nub. Ham stepped forward, stroking the beast, which continued to grow and swell beyond belief.

Paul said, "Wh-what are you gonna do with that?"

Ham said, "Daddy or sir! Don't make me remind you again!"

"Oh, sorry, Daddy. What's happening, sir?"

Ham put a reassuring hand on Paul's belly. "You'll feel it all the way up here, but it won't hurt. I'll go slowly, and as you already know, my sweet girl, everywhere my flesh touches you feels like a brilliant light in the darkness. A summer's day. The first flower of Spring."

❦

Paul was terrified. He'd never put so much as a finger up there. "No, sir. Please."

Ham smacked Paul across the face. It stung during the moment of contact, but then it felt good. Instead of the pain that follows a slap, he radiated joy and pleasure.

"Hit me again, Daddy. I was bad."

"No. You like it too much. I'll hit you when I please, little girl." With that, he grabbed Paul's feet, putting them on his shoulders. "I'm gonna fuck you now."

Paul panicked. He wriggled and resisted until he felt

the tip of the giant cock touch his butt cheeks. A powerful wave of sexual energy flowed from Ham to Paul, soothing him and making him submit.

"Daddy doesn't want you to feel bad, sissy. This is going to feel so good."

"Yes, sir. Yes, Daddy. I can feel it already."

"Move that thong out of the way. I'm coming in."

Paul obeyed.

Ham grabbed his cock mid-shaft, aiming it toward the exposed pucker. He struck home, pausing, waiting for something.

"What's wrong, Daddy? Why did you stop?"

Ham smiled. "Your pussy isn't wet enough yet. But I'll bet you can feel it getting slippery inside you."

Paul could feel something new in his ass. It was like salivating. Soon, clear droplets of juice emerged from his butthole.

"Now you're good and wet. Get ready for Daddy's dick."

Ham pressed forward, stretching the sphincter into a giant 'O'. Then the inner sphincter relaxed, allowing the enormous head to find its way into Paul's shitter.

The sensations that came next blew Paul's mind. He felt the massive cock press against his prostate. It was the first time in his life he'd felt any pressure there; it was amazing.

"Oh, shit. I mean, oh, sir."

Hamaliel glared at Paul. "Bad girl." He smacked Paul's ass. It contracted, sending even more waves of pleasure through Paul's body. He writhed in a glorious mixture of pain and joy. His teeth chattered, and his eyes fluttered.

Ham said, "Tell me how much you like it."

"Oh, Daddy, I love it. I love it, sir!"

Ham bestowed a slight smile on Paul. "That's a good girl. Daddy's little girl is a good girl."

Paul felt pressure on his bladder when Ham reached

the end of his rectum. He thought he might have to pee but knew it would anger his domineering father figure. He held it in.

"Get ready; I'm going all the way."

What came next was even more spectacular than the prostate pressure. Ham's long, thick cock found its way through the colorectal junction, making a loud popping sound as it pushed past the innermost sphincter.

Paul's eyes widened until they were saucers. Ham chuckled.

"You like that, don't you, little sissy fag."

Paul was comfortable being a girl, but he felt sudden anger at being called a fag.

"What do you mean?"

Ham smacked Paul across the face. "Don't forget, I'm your Daddy, and you will address me with respect."

"But sir, I'm a woman, not a faggot."

"You're a sissy faggot, and you love my cock in your ass, bitch."

Paul felt humiliated. "Yes, sir. I'm a sissy faggot bitch, sir."

He emphasized the word "bitch" to attempt to insult his master.

Ham snarled, revealing fangs like a wolf. "Did you just call me a bitch?"

Paul was frightened. Who was this man? Was he even a man?

"No, sir, I'm the bitch, sir. That's not what I meant, Daddy."

Ham raised a hand as if to smack his prey, but he relented. At last, his cock reached an endpoint deep inside Paul's innards. A large lump protruded next to Paul's belly button.

"Are you ready to get fucked?"

Paul nodded. "Yes, sir. Fuck me, sir."

Ham pulled back and slammed deep. The lump

moved diagonally down Paul's belly and back to its original spot on the in-stroke. "Ohhhhhh!" Paul wasn't able to say the words anymore. He waited for Ham to smack him, but the strange man was in a different place now. He was entirely concentrated on fucking Paul.

"You like that, little faggot bitch, don't you?"

Paul nodded. He managed to croak out a "yes, sir"; it was barely audible. Ham smiled.

"Tell me you're my sissy bitch." As he said these words, he sped up. The sound of his massive cock slipping in and out of the colon was like an audience of one clapping enthusiastically at the end of an opera. He fucked so fast that his lower body became a blur.

Paul heard the command and struggled to obey. It came out like a series of sentences. "I'm. Your. Sissy. Bitch. Sir." The bodily pleasure overwhelmed the straight man. He realized his cock was gushing pre-cum like a geyser.

"Your little sissy fag cunt is dripping wet. Who's making you wet, faggot?"

"You are, sir."

"That's right." Ham continued to fuck Paul faster than a jaguar running through the jungle. It hurt, but Paul was beyond pain. The strange pleasure that radiated from Ham's skin was far more powerful than any pain on earth. Paul writhed in ecstasy.

"Squeeze my cock with your boy pussy."

Paul obeyed. He tightened his sphincter around the cock. The pressure forced pussy juice out of his hole.

"That's my little bitch. Your faggot ass is just a drippy wet pussy. Isn't it."

"Yes, sir." Paul was returning to earth, concentrating on maximizing the pleasant sensations coursing through his body. He shivered, and his teeth chattered, but he was back in his body now, feeling an orgasm build in his little nub of a penis. He put his hand there, but Ham pulled it away.

"That's mine. You can't touch it, bitch."

"Sorry, sir. I won't touch it, Daddy, sir."

It turned out Paul didn't need to touch it. The orgasm crested like a wave and crashed on the shore. Despite his tiny mouse balls and rabbit dick, Paul shot a massive load. Some of it landed on Ham's face. He smacked Paul hard across the face.

"Look what you did, you fucking sissy faggot! Clean it up!" He leaned forward, close enough for Paul to lick his semen from the stranger's face. It tasted odd, like clam juice and corn syrup. Ham pulled Paul's head, their lips meeting. He kissed Paul, using his tongue to taste the same syrupy cum.

"Boy clit juice is the best. Better than pussy. I want you to make some more; you'd better warn me this time. I want it now, so you are allowed to touch that little clit. I permit you."

Paul obeyed. "Yes, Daddy." He pinched his tiny dick between his thumb and forefinger, rubbing and pinching it. To his surprise, he felt another orgasm coming on.

"I think you should open your mouth, sir. I'm gonna come again."

Ham leaned forward, mouth open wide like a Boa Constrictor. His sharp fangs terrified Paul. He wanted to scream, but he knew he'd have to stay focused so he could aim. All the while, he felt the huge cock ramming its way through him. He put one hand on his lower belly, feeling the arm-length cock forcing its way through his gut. He pressed down on his tummy, sending Ham into spasms of pleasure. The tingling of Ham's skin touching his insides increased. Paul blew an even bigger load right into Ham's mouth. He savored it before swallowing.

"Mmm. Faggot clit juice. It makes me horny." As he said these words, he sprouted small horns from his temples. Paul gasped in astonishment. Who was this beast?

Ham threw his head back. "Oh, good little faggot. You're gonna make me cum." The strange creature increased the length and speed of his strokes, causing Paul's hand to jump up and down as the lump rose beneath it.

"Here it comes. Take it, you sissy bitch." And with those words, his horns grew enormous, like a mature bull's. "Ohhhh!"

Paul felt a biblical flood of piping hot cum fill his lower intestines. It kept coming until he thought he would burst.

Ham said, "Good boy. My little sissy did good. Good little faggot."

Hearing that made Paul proud, despite the discomfort of being subjected to such degrading language. "What do you say, faggot?"

"I don't know, sir."

Ham slapped Paul hard on the ass. "You ungrateful little bitch."

Paul realized what he needed to say. "Thank you, sir. Thank you for fucking me, Daddy."

Ham nodded. "That's a good little bitch. Did you enjoy it?"

Paul said, "I loved it, sir. I never thought it could feel so good." He suddenly noticed a tail that had sprouted from Ham's backside. It swished quickly through the air, reminding Paul of the hard, fast fuck he'd just endured.

"By now, my little sissy faggot, you're probably wondering who I am."

Paul said, "I am, sir, Daddy, sir."

"I'm Hamaliel, the demon of disappointment. I grant wishes to remove your unhappiness, only to be replaced by a new sorrow."

Paul said, "But sir, I don't feel any sorrow."

Ham smiled wide, his eyes sparkling with mischief. "You will when I tell you that this is where you live now.

You'll slowly lose your mind in solitary confinement. And you're my sissy fag, no one else's. I'll come fuck you whenever I feel like it. I might lend you out to another demon as a favor. But they won't feel as good as me. Having sex with me will be the only true pleasure you'll know."

Paul felt a terrible dread wash over him. He'd been granted his wish in a strange way. He had wanted to know pleasure with a woman. He never expected that he would become the woman. He'd never felt so satisfied. But the thought of living in this windowless cell for eternity was horrifying. A few tears escaped his eyes.

"There, there, little faggot. Don't cry. My appetite for sex is enormous. You'll get plenty of fucking, and you'll never grow old, never die. And you'll come to enjoy the feel of other demons' dicks in your ass. You're a servant in Hell, and you have it better than most. There will be only the torture of isolation. No hellfire. No spikes. Just loneliness and solitude. That's not so bad, is it, little faggot?"

Paul shook his head. "No, sir. It's not bad, Daddy. It's good."

"Next time, I want you to wear the purple stockings and the golden thong, right?"

Paul nodded.

"Got that!?!?"

"Sir, yes, sir. Yes, Daddy, sir."

Ham disappeared in a puff of smoke, leaving Paul to contemplate his station in life now that he was a servant in Hell.

BOOK THREE –
CLOISTERED: FUCKING
WITH THE DEMON

by Peter Schutes

ONE MAN'S BLESSING

Vicente Pesante was a devout young boy. He lived in Guanajuato, Leon, Mexico. He attended mass every Sunday until he was old enough to join the monastery. He had grave reasons for choosing this path. In the course of his life, towards the end of his secondary school, he learned that he was not going to marry. It wasn't his plan, nor God's. It was nature itself. He just wasn't built like other men. He could never find a wife, despite his handsome face. He wasn't a hunchback and had no deformities of the spine or skull. He had all his arms, legs, fingers, and toes. No, it was a problem many men believed was a blessing: he was so well hung it was a curse. Young women in town knew of his endowment. At first, buzzing around Vicente like flies on shit, they always ran screaming in terror at the first glimpse of his enormous penis. He was angry with God and blamed him for his trouble.

Vicente's guidance counselor, Padre Ochoa, was a priest. Vicente's scowl betrayed the many dark thoughts haunting him. One day in February, Padre Ochoa hooked his arm around Vicente's.

"Come with me, son."

"Am I in trouble?" Vicente couldn't think of any transgressions.

"I believe you might be. You are angry with God, are you not?"

Vicente nodded. How did he know?

"How often do you pray?"

Vicente chuckled. "Prayer is for feeble minds."

Padre Ochoa struck him gently as if to wake him from sleep. "Open your eyes, Vicente. Prayer is for the strongest of men. Tell me what is troubling you."

Vicente adjusted his baggy trousers to be certain his shameful appendage remained hidden. "I'd rather not get into specifics."

Padre Ochoa's eyebrows raised. "It's not money, for your family has plenty. It's not looks, because you are a very handsome man. Is it a matter of the heart?"

"God has cursed me. I am deformed."

Padre Ochoa frowned. "You are delusional. You exhibit no deformity, my son."

Vicente had endured many whispers and rumors. He doubted this priest had escaped hearing them.

"Come on, Padre; you know what I mean. Surely you know what they are saying about me."

"Students rarely share their gossip with teachers. So what are they saying?"

The words weren't coming. It was impossible to speak his shame aloud. So he pulled down his pants.

Padre Ochoa's eyes were saucers. Instinctively, he grabbed the young man's cock and held it. He stroked and marveled as it went from enormous to impossible. It was bigger than a baby. The priest struggled to hold the immense slab of engorged meat.

"Mijo, you were blessed. Surely you don't doubt God's handiwork. This is a thing of beauty." Padre Ochoa planted kisses up and down its length.

Vicente shifted uncomfortably. Men aren't supposed to do this, are they? The priest pulled out his regular-sized cock from under his cassock and stroked it.

The priest tried to put the head into his mouth, but

it was impossible. His tongue swirled across the top. Vicente was a virgin. He had never felt someone do that to him. It caused a warm tingling in his belly. With each pass of the priest's tongue, something extraordinary built up in Vicente's body, like the moment at the top of the Ferris wheel when you begin to descend.

Padre Ochoa pounded his own meat with the skill of an older man. He shot his load in two minutes. But he kept going with Vicente.

Vicente was young and easily excited. Seeing the seed spill from his guidance counselor's little cock sent him over the edge. He fired round after round of hot semen down the priest's throat. Padre Ochoa gobbled it hungrily, like an infant nursing at his mother's teat. He couldn't swallow fast enough. Rivulets of semen escaped his mouth and found their way to the floor, where they joined with the many puddles of the priest's come.

Padre Ochoa wiped his mouth. "Do you still think it is a curse?"

Vicente nodded. "I would gladly trade mine for yours."

"That is a deadly sin, mijo. Envy. Be grateful for what God gave you. I know I am."

"I have tried, Father, but it makes me sad. I want a wife and children. I will never have that."

Ochoa nodded. "You're right. But I have no wife or child, and I'm very happy. Maybe you can find happiness too."

"How?"

"Pray for understanding and guidance. God will answer you."

Ⓧ 2 Ⓧ

THE GUADALAJARA BRANCH

Vicente left the counselor's office with a new attitude. He began to take time during lunch to pray in the chapel. At first, God was silent. Vicente grew angry with God again. Eventually, he noticed a peaceful feeling following his prayers. That peace was the voice of God. It began to speak to him. God told him to let go of his dreams of a happy family. He understood why he was built so strangely. God had designed him so he would naturally turn to the priesthood. He decided to go to the Jesuit seminary in Guadalajara under the Tutelage of Abbot Rábano.

It was easy to renounce his secular life and join the company of other men who, for various reasons, chose not to marry. The most common reason, he learned, was because they were attracted to other men, not women. A few were so afraid of God that they thought it was the best thing to do to ensure a happy afterlife. Then there was Vicente. He wore the robes because they covered up his shamefully large cock. Of course, living in close quarters with so many other monks meant his secret didn't remain hidden for long. In fact, on the first day, one of the monks who liked men followed him to the showers, and when he saw what Vicente was packing, he shrieked.

"What's wrong with you?" Vicente was startled and angry.

"I'm sorry. It's your dick. It's just so big."

Vicente shrugged like it was no big deal, but inside, he trembled with shame. Of course, the man told anyone and everyone about what he had seen.

"I kid you not. It's like a long, thick branch of an Ahuehuete tree."

Whispers followed Vicente everywhere he went. He was the object of so many male gazes that he felt like a hall of mirrors. It was unbearable, so he went to the Abbot for counsel.

"What is it, my son?" Even the Abbot cast surreptitious glances between Vicente's legs.

"Father, I know why God cursed me this way, but I don't know how to go on living among my brothers. It's unbearable."

The abbot nodded thoughtfully.

"Why don't you show me what you're talking about? I need a better view to be able to help you."

Vicente lifted his robes, exposing the monstrous log between his legs.

The abbot gasped. "It's too big, yes." He paused. "Do you perform the mass to purify it regularly?"

Vicente frowned. "Mass to purify?"

"Yes, my son. I think I need to teach you."

The Abbot hauled out his impressive tool. Vicente's enormous meat dwarfed it, but it would be the biggest in the room in any other setting. The senior monk grasped his cock at the base and slid his fist up and down the length. "You, too."

"But father, isn't this masturbation? It's a sin."

The Abbot glared at his acolyte. "This is a mass of purification. You must empty your semen as part of your vow of celibacy. If a layperson does this, yes, it's a sin. But we are chaste and must do this to remain so."

Vicente slowly stroked one side of his cock. His fingers could not encircle it. He had never done this before.

"Use both hands. Big strokes."

Vicente was no stranger to nocturnal emissions but had never jerked off. His orgasm in the guidance counselor's office was his only waking ejaculation. As the ritual continued, he felt the familiar tingling in his belly. It was proportional to how long, hard, and fast he stroked.

"Father, I feel funny."

"You are close to purification now. I am too."

The two men stroked themselves vigorously. The odd sensation was building in Vicente's balls and stomach. He liked how it felt. Suddenly, it grew very intense.

"Oh, Lord. What is this?"

The abbot leaped to his feet and clamped his mouth over the young man's pee hole just as Padre Ochoa had done.

Vicente thrashed with imminent orgasm, but the Abbot held the massive cock head firmly between his hands. The tongue rubbing his slit sent him over. His balls squeezed close to his groin, then his cock forced out a torrent of white-hot semen. The Abbot drank it down in greedy gulps. Then he planted his lips on him and kissed him lovingly.

"Father, why did you drink it?"

"In order to purify completely, the issue must be consumed by another man."

The Abbot held his throbbing cock close to Vicente's mouth. "Go ahead."

Vicente was barely able to engulf the head of the Abbot's cock. He found himself unconsciously sucking. The Abbot leaned back and growled.

"Take it all."

Vicente gagged when the head hit the back of his throat. Then he panicked when it passed his tonsils and wormed its way down his throat, cutting off his air supply. He was retching, and he couldn't breathe. Just when he thought he would pass out, the Abbot pulled back and let Vicente take a deep breath. An involuntary cough sent a mixture of mucus, bile, and saliva, shooting past the edges of the priest's cock.

"This is good. You are casting out demons."

Then the Abbot held the boy by the hair and forced his cock back down Vicente's throat. Without warning, he shot his load straight down Vicente's gullet. His cum was copious. As he dragged his cock back past the tonsils, Vicente felt the man splattering his mouth. It tasted like huitlacoche. But as the Abbot pulled out and sprayed the last of his load on the young man's chest and face, Vicente saw that it was as white as huitlacoche is black.

Again, they kissed. The Abbot licked some cum off of Vicente's nose.

Vicente was still hard. He wanted to force his way down the Abbot's throat, but it would be impossible.

"Abbot, I don't feel completely pure yet."

"This is because you cannot shoot straight down my throat. It may take another mass. It looks like you are ready for it now."

He was. He fed the Abbot sperm all afternoon.

The Abbot grew pensive as they shared a cigarette out on the patio.

"Father, what is it? Did I do something wrong? Is it my curse?"

The Abbot smiled and rubbed Vicente's shoulder.

"No, of course not. You have a unique gift, not a curse, and it is up to the church to determine how to manage it for you."

"Manage...how?"

"I'm going to recommend you to the Vatican short-list. It's made up of monks who have shown their devotion to Christ and are ready to become specially trained priests."

"Really? But I can't let the Pope see this."

The Abbot laughed long and loud. "If he sees it, I'll eat my hat. That man is too busy to so much as glance at a young acolyte like you. It's the Cardinals you need to watch out for. They are a treacherous lot."

"Father, wasn't what we did in your office a sin?"

"Depends on who you ask. I can't be bothered. It's like a crime with no victim."

As often happens in a young man's early life, Vicente developed feelings for his Abbot. His initiation into the purification mass made him feel an intense bond, And the flavor of his cum was intoxicating. Mass took place every Wednesday night after Vespers and every Saturday morning before breakfast. With each encounter, Vicente became more attached to this strong father figure. So, when the news came that Vicente was going to Rome, his joy was trumped with sorrow. He held himself together during the announcement and the dinner that followed, but then he ran to his quarters and sobbed. He felt a familiar hand caress his shoulder.

"Why the tears, Son? Are you frightened?"

"I...I don't know what this is. I think I love you. I don't want to go to Rome. I want to be with you all the time."

"This is puppy love. It feels real, but it's not. We have an arrangement on Wednesdays and Saturdays. Brother Pedro and I have an arrangement on Tuesday morning after mass. It's just that: an arrangement. Nothing more."

Vicente turned red. "You can't tell me that all those kisses meant nothing."

"They're just to keep us in the mood. It's not love, Vicente. I promise you. As a priest, you may someday find love with a fellow clergyman, but you mustn't fall in love with the laity. And when you find love, you will know. Whatever your heart is feeling now for me will be multiplied a hundredfold.

3

FRENCH KISS

Vicente took a bus to Veracruz, where he caught a Steamship bound for Le Havre. He had learned enough French to get by. He was two days from Rome by train. He wasn't to be there until the following week. So he had time to kill. In Le Havre, along the waterfront, were a host of establishments catering to sailors. Loud women drank big mugs of beer and sat on the sailors' laps. Having a woman sit on his lap was an unpleasant image. She would discover the monstrosity under his robes and scream. She would spill her beer down the front of his cassock. It was not what he wanted at all.

Vicente looked for a hotel near the train station. In doing so, he passed a bar full of sailors with no women in sight. He was thirsty. A beer sounded good to him. The Bar was called "Le Dragon Rouge." It was poorly lit. The sailors sat close. Vicente saw two men in British Navy uniforms who drew closer to one another until they finally kissed. Vicente was instantly turned on. His robe began to tent outward. He turned away, desperate for a hiding place, but nothing could hide what was growing under there.

There were whistles and cries of "Sacre Bleu!" In less than a minute, he was the most popular man in the bar. Sailors and servants knelt before the almighty phallus. For the first time, Vicente had more than one mouth on his cock. Like piglets nursing, they all fought for a spot on his cock. Even the bartender came out from behind the bar and knelt in reverence. This was a mass unlike any he'd enjoyed with the Abbot. This was brazen, out in the open, and open to all. Vicente showered his admirers with an unending supply of cum. It saturated the hair of the men kneeling before him. The men, in turn, shot their loads on the floor. The ground grew slick underfoot. Loyal worshippers brought damp bar towels to wipe down the floor, only to see it covered in a thick new layer of seamen's semen.

More than one man reached around and touched Vicente's asshole. He jumped each time. It didn't feel unpleasant, just surprising. When a spit-soaked finger wriggled its way in, pain caused his knees to buckle. But the finger hit paydirt. It pressed and wriggled against Vicente's prostate gland. Immediately, he shot another load, perhaps his fifth. The finger massaged further until clear juices ran from his spent cock. Vicente had discovered the sexual potential buried in that hole and wanted to learn more.

Spent, he staggered out of the bar and into the nearest hotel. He could only stay one night before catching his train to Paris, then on to Rome via Milan. In Paris, he looked in vain for a bar like Dragon Rouge but found none near the Gare de Lyon.

As he waited in the station for his train, drinking a Coca-Cola, he noticed more men entering the toilet than coming out. He needed to pee anyway, so he checked his bags at Left Luggage and explored the WC. It was an open-air orgy to rival the Dragon Rouge. Men of all shapes, sizes, and colors stood at the urinals performing mass. When they saw Vicente's collar, there was a pause in the action. If Vicente had turned tail and run out, they would have assumed he was going to the gendarmes. But he stood his ground, smiling. So, the orgy continued. Vicente wore his robes, so the mystery had yet to be revealed. People left him alone. Who wants to fuck a priest? But when Vicente stepped forward and hauled out his meat to take a piss, the room uttered a collective gasp. He couldn't keep them off it. At least ten men sucked on different parts of his cock. Then a whistle blew. Everyone stood and put away their privates, and in a herd, they fled the restroom, leaving Vicente abandoned. He wasn't sure if the cop had seen what was under Vicente's robes.

"Vous êtes en état d'arrestation. You are under ze arrest."

In handcuffs, Vicente pleaded with the cop, who didn't believe he was a priest. He told the policeman that he had finished a Coke and needed to pee. He didn't know what was going on. The men assaulted him. The gendarme shrugged.

"Tell it to the judge."

Vicente was enraged. "The great judge will sentence you, my friend, and when they see you falsely arrested a priest, he'll see you fry in hell. Fire and brimstone will surround you. You will burn for an eternity. I will pray for you, but it won't help."

The cop hesitated. He leaned close to the priest and whispered, "I'll let you go if you let me play with it."

"Is this a trap?"

"No. Come with me."

The cop let Vicente collect his luggage and brought him into the tiny police station inside the Gare de Lyon. There was nobody there.

"I'm Jean-Pierre." The handsome cop removed his shirt, revealing a massive chest and bulging biceps.

"Vicente. Padre Vicente." He wasn't a Padre yet, but it helped his case.

"Padre, I want you to rub your prick on my nipples. Yeah?"

Vicente nodded. "Please, could you remove these handcuffs?" Despite his fear, the young seminarian could feel the blood rushing to his cock, causing it to swell and point outward.

The cop smiled. He released Vicente, who shook his wrists to reduce the cramping. Jean-Pierre faced his quarry. "Now you will rub your hard cock on my nipples."

"You'll need to back up."

The cop laughed until Vicente revealed his meat pole. "Oh, you were not kidding." Jean-Pierre took two steps back, then three. Vicente caressed the cop's nipples with the head of his massive cock. He drew invisible circles on his pectoral muscles. It felt nice to be so close to another man like this.

The cop gave Vicente a rough shove. He landed on a desk. The cop gripped his legs and held them aloft. "I will fuck your ass now."

The cop coated his growing cock in saliva. Vicente hoped the Frenchman was hung small, but he wasn't. As Jean-Pierre grew harder, it became clear that Vicente was in for a world of pain. The cop put his long, thick cock at the entry and gently pushed. He added more spit. "You are very tight."

Vicente nodded. "I've never done this." Suddenly, he saw a blinding flash of white light. His ass throbbed then cramped as the police officer pushed his fuck stick deep inside the Mexican. Vicente howled and pounded the desk, but it was no use. The policeman was determined to have his prize. Despite Vicente's pleas, the man just kept pushing forward. He reached the end of Vicente's rectum, then paused there. He still had a few inches to go, but he waited with the patience every well-hung top man knows. He sighed impatiently.

The cramps subsided; a warm, rhythmic pleasure replaced the pain. The cop held fast, waiting for the green light. Vicente gave a quick nod. The gendarme seesawed back and forth, sending Vicente into a miasma of pleasure, pain, and arousal. He put his hands together on either side of his own cock and began the ritual he had been taught. Jean-Pierre sent shivers of pain down Vicente's spine, with each thrust hitting the back wall of his ass hard.

The cop pushed hard against the back of Vicente's rectum until, with great force, he turned the corner and pushed past into the colon.

"Did you tear a hole in me? Am I going to die?"

The policeman smiled. "Relax. It is only your valve. I have straightened it and can push past now." Each time he did, Vicente's eyes rolled back, and he let out a soft moan.

The Frenchman gave Vicente a glassy stare. He was on another plane. He whispered in French. "Oui, oui mon prête."

The pain returned. Vicente tried to push the cop away. Jean-Pierre withdrew and slicked up his cock with generous amounts of spit before pushing back in. The pain was gone entirely. Vicente lay back, stroking his one-of-a-kind massive cock, eyelids fluttering. He loved how the thick cock head pressed on his prostate, then invaded his digestive tract.

As the Frenchman drew close to orgasm, he released a scent that caused Vicente to dribble clear precum on his face. Each thrust was a new level of ecstasy. Vicente had never known he could be with another man this way. It was like a very addictive drug. He wasn't even done, and he wanted more.

"Ah, OUI! OUI!". The Frenchman ejaculated hard, coating Vicente's insides with warm semen.

The knowledge that his insides had just made another man cum, coupled with the slippery warmth inside him, was too much. The orgasm started deep inside where the Frenchman had spattered him with cum, and moved in ripples of ecstasy to the root of his cock, where he began firing the biggest load since he learned the ritual back in high school. It shot past his head and onto the far wall of the office, over and over, leaving puddles of ejaculate along the trajectory. The last drops dribbled out and fell onto his face.

Vicente was startled when the cop licked the semen from his face and planted his lips on the priest's. The officer's tongue darted about inside Vicente's mouth. Vicente liked this feeling, even with the French officer's body crushing the goliath of a cock between them. With an involuntary peristaltic push, Vicente ejected the cop's soft penis along with a small ocean of semen and a long, loud fart.

Vicente's eyes strayed across the clock.

"Is that correct?"

"Eh, oui. It's nineteen with ten minutes."

"My train leaves in five minutes! I don't even know which track."

The gendarme helped Vicente with his luggage. They located the train on a track on the far side of the station. The train whistle blew while they were halfway to the platform. As they rounded the platform, the train began to pull out. The gendarme blew his whistle rapidly five times. The train slowed, then stopped. Vicente climbed aboard, saluted the officer, and made his way to the second-class compartment where he would be sleeping.

4

CABIN FEVER

The cabins were all full, six passengers each. The beds were hidden in the walls. Vicente told a white lie - he said his back was injured, and he needed to use the bottom bunk. The truth was, he knew that someone would see his embarrassing appendage if he had to climb or descend a higher bunk.

The five other men in his cabin were solid, Italian working-class types. They were delighted to have a priest on board. It was considered incredibly lucky. Vicente was tuckered out after all the action he had seen in the past few days. He took some time to reflect. It was clear that men wanted him, and they had much to offer as well. They were willing to submit to it or else try to take him and thereby claim the prize as part of their conquest. When the conductor came to turn down the beds, he stared at Vicente. He wasn't looking at the region below his waist; he was looking him right in the eyes.

Vicente smiled and introduced himself. The conductor blushed.

"I'm sorry, it's just that I have never seen a face so exotic. Are you Moroccan?"

Vicente laughed. "I'm from Mexico."

The conductor was unusually quiet. Once everyone

was settled in their bunks, he leaned down to the priest in his tiny bed.

"Father, my name is Arsenault. I need to talk to you."

Vicente was exhausted, but when the Lord called, he always answered.

"Do you have someplace private?"

The conductor nodded. He had his own room at the back of the train. It looked the same size as a first-class cabin but had none of the fine trimmings.

Arsenault was probably five years older than young Vicente.

"Son, what is troubling you?"

The conductor turned pink. His ears burned, and a vein in his neck pulsed visibly.

"Father, I'm a deviate."

"A what?"

"A sodomite. I have sex with men."

Vicente looked at the ring on the man's finger.

"Does she know?"

He shook his head, fighting back tears.

"Do you enjoy having sex with men?"

The Frenchman opened his eyes wide. "I don't, er, I never thought about it. It's bad. I'm going to hell."

"Don't you keep doing it because you feel pleasure?"

The man's head hung down as he nodded.

Vicente could see the effects of his church on this poor man. It wasn't right.

"Arsenault, I am going to tell you a secret. You must promise to keep it and only share it with others like yourself. God doesn't care what you do in bed. He doesn't care who you do it with, so long as you're both adults and you both want it."

This was a revelation for the big pink Frenchman. His eyes fell below Vicente's waist. He saw something puzzling down there.

"Is this you?" He gestured at a strange protrusion under the cloth.

Vicente was brown, so blushing didn't show as it did on European faces. But he was crimson.

The conductor, dazzled by the enormity, reached out and grabbed hold somewhere near the knee. He stroked it with increasing intensity until it began to rise. "God has blessed you, Father."

Vicente smirked. "Too much of a good thing is bad."

The conductor moved aside the robe to marvel at the entire package. It was the size of a grown man's arm. "There are men who could take it. I have met them in Paris at the Turkish baths."

Vicente shook his head. "You're imagining things."

The conductor stroked himself as he talked with the priest. "Some men can take an entire arm to the shoulder."

Vicente's mind reeled. This couldn't be true. The sexual chemistry was off between him and the conductor. Vicente was no more than a pornographic image for the man to worship.

"I am always French active and Greek passive. I could neither suck you nor let you fuck me. Oh! Pardon my foul language."

Vicente smiled. "Such language is necessary when describing acts of intimacy. Don't be troubled."

The conductor had a small penis. His hand covered it completely. He used two fingers and his thumb. He walked to the sink and shot his load. He rinsed it down with hot water.

Vicente wasn't aroused. He put his cock away and stood.

"Father, thank you. You've made me a happier man. God bless you."

Vicente returned to his cabin, where everyone had fallen asleep. He slipped in as quietly as possible, catching his cock on the door jamb. Someone coughed.

It was the man across from him on the other lower bunk.

As Vicente climbed under the covers, the man whispered to him. "Did I just see that?"

Vicente was so tired of being a zoo animal. But he practiced tolerance and patience everywhere he went. "Yes, I believe so."

"May I see?"

It was all too easy for Vicente to lift his skirt and give the man a glimpse.

"Mamma Mia!" He said it loud enough to wake another passenger in the bunk above him.

"Shh!" The man said, but he couldn't miss the impressive display in Vicente's bunk.

He clamped his hand over his mouth to keep from shouting.

The man directly across from Vicente already had his cock out and was rubbing it furiously. The fellow above him wasted no time, drawing sexual energy from the magic totem that was Vicente's enormous cock. Italian men could be very well hung. Three of the men sported giant thick poles that would please even the most craven woman or man. The other two were the opposite, with little penises the size of a pinky. The whole cabin, including Vicente, had a wank. After six ejaculations shot skyward and then fell to the floor, a house painter passed around clean shop towels so they could all sponge themselves and the floor. Vicente wanted to put away his prize pony, but there were a few men who had another one in them. He slept with his cock exposed for the benefit of his cabin mates. He woke several times because men couldn't keep their hands off it.

In the morning, the men couldn't look Vicente in the eye. They were fighting off the shame that prevailed in Catholic countries like Mexico, France, and Italy.

The train was past Turin, due to arrive in Milan in

another hour. Vicente brushed his teeth and washed his face. He cleaned cum out of his hair and off of his cock. The cum was not all his own.

The Milan Central train station was beautiful. It was the biggest train station he had ever seen. In Paris, the train stations were split between North, South, East, and West. Milan Central was all of these.

Vicente had traveler's dyspepsia. Something he ate had disagreed with him. He urgently needed a bathroom. He had no trouble spotting them, but Vicente was taken aback when he entered.

There were several problems with this restroom. First, a few men were hanging out with their pants down to their knees. They sported erections and were taking turns admiring each other. Second, the toilets had no doors. The last problem was the toilets themselves. They were Turkish, which meant there was no seat. To defecate, a man had to squat close to the ground and aim for the hole between his feet. Many people had poor aim. Vicente would soil his robe and get his dick dirty in the muck. It was acceptable for normal men in pants. It was a nightmare for a priest in robes with a 14-inch beast dangling down. He hoisted his robes onto his shoulders, then dangled his cock over his knee to keep it from touching the filthy porcelain. Despite Vicente's pleas to leave him in peace, a crowd gathered to look at the colossus. He grew angry as the hungry vultures circled while he farted and blasted burning diarrhea out of his unhappy hole. Not even the foul odor could keep them from staring slack-jawed at the eighth wonder of the world. He squatted there long enough for several men to ejaculate on him. At last, the stomach cramps subsided. He stood and let the robe fall to his ankles. Swiftly, he pushed past the energy vampires and out onto the platform. The most brazen men followed him until he turned and shouted, "Maledetti fantasmi, averanno fame per l'eternitá!" [Accursed ghosts, you will be hungry forever]. It worked. Italians believe in ghosts and curses, especially coming from a man of the cloth. Soon he was alone with his secret again. The robes concealed everything. He had a long, peaceful train ride to Termini Station in Rome.

The rail and transit system had fallen into organized chaos after the war. A casual traveler always left the station bewildered. It should be so easy to get to Vatican City from there. Still, each person he asked had different advice, always involving getting off at the Piazza Argentina or Campo dei Fiori and flagging down a series of buses and taxis. Finally, a sensible old woman in a smart Chanel suit pointed him to the electric trolleys. One went directly to St. Peter's. He didn't understand her last bit of advice.

Once he got on, he realized why the other suggestions were so much more complicated. This simple direct line was far too popular to handle the volume of passengers needing it. The car filled to capacity and beyond. An old man with a sadistic smile was crushed against Vicente's manhood. He brazenly lifted the sacred robe and stroked him. Vicente was trapped in place. At each stop, more people tried to get on. The old man was talented with his hands. He got Vicente hard as a rock and stroked him to climax just in time to disembark at St. Peter's. The old man's shoes were patent leather, black and shiny, were it not for Vicente's cum. The priest was startled by the depravity but intrigued by the possibilities it foretold. If all Roman men were this horny, it would be quite a carnival ride. But Rome was nothing compared to Vatican City.

5

THE POPE'S HOUSE

The Vatican is a nation-state. As such, it has its own stamps and passports and enforces Papal law rather than Italian law. Trying to print their own money is inconvenient, so they have settled for the Italian Lira. A line of nuns and priests waited patiently to enter the city at the entrance behind St. Peter's. At the front of the line, in the entryway, stood a colorfully dressed man resembling both a court jester and a soldier. He was an officer in the Swiss Guard, the Vatican army. When at last it was his turn, Vicente presented his passport. The guard nodded and consulted a clipboard full of names.

"Ah, yes, I do remember. You are to meet with Cardinale Beluomo at suppertime. Your room is two floors below San Pietro. Number 96. We dine at eight." The guard thrust a set of keys into Vicente's palm.

After dozens of wrong turns, Vicente found himself in front of number 96. He made the sign of the cross before opening his door. The room was charmingly medieval. The only decoration was a simple bed, smooth tan walls, and a row of candle holders. Vicente noticed with alarm that there was no bathroom attached.

Like many men, Vicente had a phobia of group showers. For the masses of men whose endowment was within an inch of average, it was a place to compare and see where one stood on the spectrum of penis size. Vicente was so much bigger than any man he'd ever seen, by more than six inches in length and girth. He couldn't casually enter a communal shower without causing a panic.

To set his mind at ease, Vicente searched for the commode and showers, hoping for privacy. No, the toilets were just like the station in Milan. No doors, and Turkish style. He heard the sound of running water and found the showers. Every shower head was taken, and a half dozen men waited patiently, towels wrapped tightly around their waists. Vicente groaned without realizing he did so aloud. The man closest to him, a beautiful blue-eyed blond with shiny white teeth, smiled.

"I get it. I hate ze showers like zo. My schwanz is too kleine." He opened his towel and let Vicente see his modest penis. "Are you alzo kleine? Small?"

Vicente shook his head. "No, I have the opposite problem."

The blond priest's smile faded. "I don't understand."

With a quick glance to be sure no one was paying him any attention, Vicente stretched his robe, revealing a partial outline of his cock, but not entirely giving away its actual size.

The tow-headed Swiss German swooned and made the sign of the cross. "God has given you a gift."

Vicente sighed. It was the devil, more likely. He excused himself to go pee. He rejoiced that when standing facing inward, the toilet stall was relatively private. He could lift the front of his robe and allow his cock to dangle below his knees. With such a short distance to go, he had remarkable aim. He noticed the other men had piss on their shoes and ankles, caused by the splash-back when they missed the target.

After thoroughly shaking the piss out of the long passageway between his balls and the tip, Vicente returned to his room. He read from the bible until it was time to meet Cardinale Beluomo for supper.

Many arrows guided Vicente to the dining room. He wasn't sure how he would find his way back, but he spied the beautiful blond boy eating and chatting with his friends. He waved. "Halloo! Come eat with us!"

"I'm meeting someone." Vicente didn't want to shout.

"Was ist das? I cannot hear you!"

Vicente strolled over to the table. It was clear from the disinterested expression on his friends' faces that he had not given away Vicente's secret. 'Thank heaven for small mercies,' Vicente thought to himself.

"I am Hans. Hans Klein." The beautiful priest extended his hand.

"Vicente Pesante."

"Won't you join us?"

"I'm afraid I can't. Not tonight. I have a meeting with Cardinale Beluomo."

A few whispers and giggles passed between the friends of Hans.

"My friend, I am sorry you must start off like that. Beluomo is a wolf in sheep's clothing. Be careful what you say."

"Is he here yet?"

Hans laughed. "The cardinals don't dine in the cafeteria; you must go to his chambers. Schnell. You mustn't be late!"

Vicente saw he had three minutes to find the Cardinal's quarters. He rushed through hallways asking directions like a madman. As the bells of St Peter's struck eight, Vicente knocked beneath a faceplate that read "Cardinale Beluomo."

The door opened to reveal a very handsome man with dark hair and smoldering brown eyes. The Cardinal smiled warmly. "Come in. You must be Vicente."

The Cardinal's suite was much larger and had an adjoined bathroom. A small feast weighed down the dining table.

"You must be starving. Eat. Eat." The two men could hardly see one another for all the food between them. There were game hens, roast beef, ham, fruits, and cheeses - more than Vicente could eat in a week.

After eating considerably more than he should have, Vicente felt sleepy. His head nodded.

"Ah-ah-ah. We need you awake, my child. It's time for Vespers."

Vicente followed Cardinale Beluomo to the small chapel below the Basilica. As Vicente walked in, the room came to life with whispers and stares. The Cardinal threw a stern look at the many high-ranking officials. They sat in a comfortable pew and recited evening prayers. The kneelers were upholstered with soft velvet, a solid contrast to the unadorned kneelers in Guadalajara.

It was after Vespers that Vicente's world turned upside down. The Vatican brass left the chapel by a different door than Vicente had entered. His fellow priests followed. He joined the throng. The door led to a downward sloped passageway, then down several sets of stairs. The metal gave way to wood, then clay with each successive staircase. They arrived at an ancient structure, older than Rome itself.

"What is this place?"

The Cardinal grinned. "It is the true seat of worship." The lintel above the door was inscribed in symbols beyond Vicente's recognition.

"What does it say?"

"This is the temple of Asmodeus, the ruler of Sensuality and Pleasure."

They entered the small structure. It was dark inside. The Cardinal said, "You shall tell no other living man what has happened here tonight."

A chorus of voices repeated; Vicente stumbled

through the words. His eyes were adjusting to the darkness. He saw the high-ranking officials disrobing. What were they doing? From the ceiling were suspended leather hammocks with stirrups. The younger men climbed into the hammocks and put their feet in the stirrups. The cardinal nudged Vicente.

"Go on, take your place."

Vicente took off his robe and reluctantly lay in the prone position, his feet supported by the stirrups. His cock covered his face, so he pushed it to one side.

The oldest man, whose hands quaked like parchment in the Tehuano Winds, hobbled around the circle of slings and applied lard to the holes of the young men. He paused when he saw Vicente's monstrosity. He grinned in approval before liberally applying the slippery shortening to Vicente's rear end.

The Cardinal stood before him. To Vicente's horror, he saw the man possessed a very thick cock the size and length of a can of frijoles. The young priest stole glances at the other men. None were as thick as Beluomo, though many were longer. The cardinal pressed against his hole. As he pushed the tip part way in, Vicente was overcome with pain. He uttered an involuntary cry for help. He could hear others doing the same.

Nobody fucked yet. They were all poised and slightly inside the boys but stayed in place. The trembling old man was not a participant in the sex. Instead, he brought around glasses of warm honey mead with botanical extracts. It was like cough syrup but tasted better. The older men, poised for sexual thrusts, were given a different concoction that caused their cocks to swell even further. Vicente was terrified, but suddenly nothing mattered anymore as the honey mead took effect. The walls of the ancient temple began to melt.

Somewhere far below his head, the Cardinal forced his way into Vicente's flesh. Vicente was caught in a dream state, where he was visited by his sexual partners from the recent past. The Cardinal just reached the end of the rectum. He pounded Vicente, who felt a rising tide of pleasure engulf him and wash him out to a sea of anal sex. His lips were numb, as were his extremities. The pain that he could hardly feel connected with his pleasure center. Suddenly, every thrust, every pounding of Cardinale Beluomo's brutal cock was like its own orgasm. Vicente's cock stood straight up, swaying like an inverted pendulum with each cruel stroke. Vicente used both hands to wipe his buttocks. They were covered in blood and lard. He spit in his palms. With long, gentle strokes, he used his hands to masturbate.

The cardinal approved. "Si, piccolino, fatti la sega." Vicente didn't know what it meant, but he could tell he was doing as he should.

Around the room, whimpers and moans mingled with grunts and curses. One by one, the older men popped off, filling their partners. Vicente and his cohort of young acolytes were still immune to pain, seeing visions and writhing with pleasure. Every nerve in Vicente's body was infected with ecstatic joy. The Cardinal didn't cum easily. He was the last. When he finally ejaculated deep inside Vicente, the cum had nowhere to go. It sprayed back out past the Cardinal's thick cock.

"Che fica stretta!" he shouted. Vicente knew this meant tight pussy but didn't know how.

With Cardinale Beluomo's cry, the ceremony shifted. The old man passed out more drinks for the older men. They rotated like a clock. The man who stood before Vicente was a bundle of muscles and a beard. He looked like Hercules. Vicente saw he had a large but not huge cock. When the Greek Demigod saw Vicente's massive pole, he whistled.

"Crikey! That's a big bonk-on." He touched it and shivered. "You must have scared 'em off."

Vicente nodded. He was in a state of bliss. The man could ask him anything, and he would agree.

"Tell you what," said the muscular man with the Australian accent, "I've got a mind to try it myself."

Vicente nodded

"Good. You won't be disappointed. I can take a man's arm." He took a lump of lard and put it inside his asshole.

When the fucking began, the muscle man picked up the younger priest and brought him to a dark corner, laying him on a blanket. Vicente was flying on a magic carpet.

The Aussie priest stood on tiptoes and slipped the first inch of Vicente inside him. Vicente had never experienced this sensation. A tongue felt very different from a warm slippery hole. The older priest held his breath and squatted down. His cock stood straight out, throbbing. He was turned on, and Vicente could see it. Three more inches of cock slipped in until a loud pop told Vicente that the head was in.

"Blimey! It's a monster, though."

"It's okay if you want to stop."

The Australian muscleman frowned at him. "I got this far; I'm still crackin' a fatty. I ain't about to throw in the towel." Vicente was glad the man didn't want to stop. "If you see me lose my fatty, you'll know I'm crying uncle."

Vicente leaned back and allowed the pleasure to caress him like a pinata in the wind. The Aussie had reached the end of the rectum. He twisted until the cock pushed past the valve with a loud slap. "Holy Mary, Mother of Christ and the little fishes! Oh my God. Dear lord!" Vicente had never felt the inside of a man before. He throbbed with pleasure, growing thicker inside the poor holy man.

"You're gonna split me in two!" The Aussie kept pushing, inch by inch until his sigmoid colon finally filled to capacity. He had an inch to go. The last inch must have touched a nerve, in a good way. "Woooo! I believe! Hallelujah!" Seated on Vicente's lap, he leaned forward until his hard nipples grazed against Vicente's skin. Then he gave the lad a bear hug. It was electric. Vicente felt the incredible power and tolerance for pain that had allowed the muscle man to achieve his goals. He felt the power grow even stronger when the man slid up and down Vicente's pole. He knew how to accommodate large objects. Each time he let the head of Vicente's cock slide out of the colon, his eyes fluttered. Vicente felt intense pleasure – far more potent than masturbation. This was the mass he had dreamed of.

The Australian was in a trance. His eyes were glassy. He muttered, "Yeah. Oh Yeah." repeatedly like a prayer. Without warning, he shot a massive load of cum across Vicente's chest and face.

"You did that, brother." He leaned forward, but instead of a mere bear hug, he gave Vicente a passionate kiss. The scent of the man, the honey mead, the lips connecting – they formed a symphony that caused Vicente to unleash a flood deep in the man's colon.

With Vicente still buried inside him, they returned to the sling.

"Go ahead, fuck me yourself." Vicente could see a gleam in the man's eye. Out of this dark corner, he could see how this priest could give Steve Reeves a run for his money. He was so macho, virile, strong. It made Vicente want to provide him with more pleasure. He thrust his hips back and forth, first in small strokes, then with longer ones, until his head nearly popped out before thrusting past the curve, causing a loud smacking sound. The Aussie moaned each time. His cock was rock hard, throbbing from the assault on his innards. Vicente fucked the man with wild abandon. At one point, he buried himself to the root, which caused his muscular partner to shoot another load. Vicente felt a burning in his belly that he had grown to recognize as the point of no return. He thrust harder, more rapidly, until a burning hot orgasm rushed out of his balls and coated the Aussie's insides. The kiss lasted five minutes when the bell tolled midnight. The ceremony was over.

There were groans of disappointment which Vicente realized were coming from disappointed men who wanted a go at him.

"How often does this happen, Cardinal Highsmith?"

The cardinal grinned. "Every night, mate. Every night."

❧ 6 ❧

THE GILDED CAGE

It turned out that the Australian was not joking. It seemed the Catholic Church was obliged to Asmodeus, a demon who only spoke in the language of all-male orgies, hallucinogens, and bacchanalia. When the language of man was required, there was an oracle. The frail older man with parchment hands would ingest some herb from the Amazon forest and spout prophecies and orders from Asmodeus. It seemed the demon was pleased by Vicente's hyper-phallic prowess.

One night, in a stupor, the old man said, "Among you is a novitiate with a harpoon to rival all others. I will be sated only when he has pierced each of you and left his manly issue deep inside." There were terrified faces on the other novitiates and many of the Cardinals. The oracle chuckled.

"I suggest you practice with fists and elbows. And it would be best if you kept this novitiate in chambers so that he only fraternizes with those present, the Acolytes.

This changed Vicente's life completely. He was moved from the common floor to a large suite, bigger than Cardinal Beluomo's. He had juvenile servants to attend to his robes and bath.

The posh surroundings disguised his captivity. There were iron grates on the window. He was not permitted to dine in the cafeteria or even leave the floor where he was imprisoned. He was permitted to request books from the Vatican Library. He secured copies of the *Malleus Maleficarum* and *The Lesser Key of Solomon*. Although little was revealed about the demon, he learned of his Sigil, an intricate medallion-shaped drawing that could summon "Asmoday" by night. With great care, Vicente traced the design until he had mastered it.

Every night, a new novitiate was made the sacrificial lamb. Hands stretched their holes until they no longer closed but instead gaped wide open. Then Vicente was forced to enter them, despite their pleas and cries for mercy. During the ritual, the old man gave him an elixir that took hold of his cock and kept it rock solid, even after orgasm. The look of terror on the younger men often transformed into bliss. A satisfied smile would stretch across their face, and their eyes would flutter and roll. This was Vicente's cue to start fucking in earnest. He was thrilled to know what it meant to be on top finally. The masculine energy coursed through him, so different from the feminine energy when he had been the passive one. He had taken his rightful place in the hierarchy of male sex.

Despite these positive benefits, Vicente knew he was a slave. Like a stallion consigned as a stud, he had to fuck every hole in sight. He couldn't leave his luxurious prison. He could order a massage or demand anything for dinner, but he had to stay in his room. He only left for Vespers and the Asmodean bacchanalia that followed. A Swiss Guard was permanently stationed on his floor, preventing him from leaving his room. He was a bull in a gilded bullpen.

This sexual slavery continued day in and day out until Vicente lost track of the calendar. He carved notches in his headboard to count the days. When that ran out of space, he started on the nightstand.

One day, while Vicente soaked in a giant bathtub, Hans knocked on his door.

"What are you doing here?" Vicente pulled the tow-headed youth out of the hallway and slammed his door.

"I came to ask you the same question." Vicente only wore robes to Vespers and spent most of his time naked. The servants didn't like it, but they were his servants, so too bad. Because he didn't know who was at the door, he'd wrapped himself in a towel and a bathrobe to hide what he could. Hans didn't fully know his secret.

"I'm on a special committee. The Asm...the uh, Asmodean Council."

Hans was fascinated. "What do you do? Why do I never see you in the dining room?"

Vicente couldn't let Hans find out about his nightly orgies in the sub-sub-basement of St. Peter's. It was a deadly secret.

"I am busy preparing for council activities. They bring food to my room." As if on cue, a young servant entered and placed a small banquet on the large table.

Hans frowned. "Something is not right." Vicente knew that servants were spies. He held a finger over the young man's lips until the young snitch left. It would be awful if the servant told the Cardinals about a guest in his room. He didn't want them to hear what he said next.

"Hans, I'm a prisoner here."

"What did you do wrong?"

Vicente shook his head. "This." He let the towel drop, revealing himself entirely. Moments later, Hans hit the floor, unconscious.

When Hans came to, Vicente helped him to the couch. The blond boy stared fixedly, his mouth opening and closing in small movements. "May I touch it?"

Vicente shrugged. Hans stroked a portion of the log-like penis that swayed before his eyes. Vicente was bored by men's fascination with his anatomy, but Hans was a kind person who made him feel welcome. It was both tender and arousing.

Soon the elephantine cock swelled and lifted. Hans pulled his hands away. "Why do they keep you locked up?"

Vicente couldn't let an outsider know the truth beneath St. Peter's. "My cock is obscene before the eyes of Christ. I mustn't go where it can be seen."

Hans shook his head. "No, it's something to do with your role in the council. What is Asmodea anyway?"

Hans was too clever.

"If I tell you the truth, your life may be in danger."

Hans returned to petting Vicente's massive member. "I love a mystery! Intrigue! Spies!"

"How did you find me?"

"I asked around." Hans smiled broadly. "A busboy in the cafeteria knew your name. He told me in exchange for a blowjob."

"How did you get past the guard?"

Vicente held up an important-looking badge. "This."

"What is it?"

"A toy policeman's badge, with some minor alterations." They both chuckled.

"Well, have you seen enough? Heard enough?"

Again, Hans smiled. "No. What is the Asmodean Council?"

Vicente thought, "Oh, what the hell." He said, "Hans, if I tell you this secret, you must not gossip or whisper a word to anyone. Not one word."

Hans nodded.

"I mean it. Look me in the eyes when you say it."

Hans tore his eyes from Vicente's cock and locked gazes with the Mexican. "I solemnly swear I will not tell a soul about this secret, no matter what it may be."

As Vicente recounted the events since his first Vespers, Hans grew restless.

"This is blasphemy. Why are you saying that Pius XII worships demons?"

"One Demon. Asmodeus. It's true."

Hans shook his head. "No, I refuse to believe it. You are pranking me. Besides, no man could take that - that thing. You would kill him."

Vicente regretted his choice to come clean. "You're right, Hans; I'm pranking you."

The German grew pensive. "It is too detailed to come from your imagination. Who said, 'When all other possibilities have been eliminated, whatever remains, no matter how far-fetched, must be the truth.'?

Vicente answered, "Sir Arthur Conan Doyle."

Hans snapped his fingers. "Yes, Sherlock Holmes. You told me a few reasons for your imprisonment, swore me to secrecy, then told me a highly improbable tale. I doubted you until you chose to renege."

"The most important piece is your promise," Vicente said. "You will die if anyone learns of your knowledge."

Hans made the sign for a lock turning across his lips. He threw away the invisible key. "Now, we must find a way to get you out of here. But first, I thought of how you could prove your story to me. You must fuck me."

Hans lifted his robes and knelt on the sofa, exposing a hairless pink butthole. I have had a hand in me before. I maybe can do it.

Vicente feared for the little man's life. Not only was he in danger of internal bleeding, but he was also stealing semen from Asmodeus. His cock decided for him. Seeing the beautiful pink butthole in his sunlit room made him grow huge and hard. He throbbed with anticipation at the entryway to bliss. He lifted a narrow clay jar of olive oil from the nearby banquet table. He applied it liberally to his throbbing cock, then handed it to Hans, who inserted it quickly before upending it. He was ready.

Vicente pressed on the flesh gateway until Hans bit a pillow and screamed. He waited there patiently, just an inch or less in. He grew much thicker further down, so Hans needed loosening. He pushed some more. Hans breathed rapidly, clutching his little rock-hard penis to prevent the clear trail of liquid from staining the velvet sofa.

"Keep going," Hans said. "Don't be afraid of hurting me."

Vicente was anxious to feel this young man encircling his entirety. He nudged hard, and his head popped audibly as it entered the rectum. Now it was easy. Vicente drove his cock forward until it reached the first fold. He pushed again and reached the second crease. After that, he slid forward to the bend. He waited.

Hans nodded. Vicente straightened the bend and filled the colon. He hit the descending colon, and the young priest had an involuntary orgasm that soaked the velvet couch. At last, Vicente was inside completely. Hans looked over his shoulder, smiling. "Fuck me, my friend."

Vicente battered his way in and out, causing the German to scream into his pillow a second time, then a third. When Hans turned to look over his shoulder, Vicente saw sweat and tears. "My friend," Hans said, "I want to look you in the eye. Let's do it like Mommy and Daddy."

Vicente lifted the boy and rotated him around so he lay on his back. Because Hans was so thin, Vicente could see the outline of the giant cock as it wormed its way through the boy's lower digestive tract. Their eyes locked. Hans reached up and pinched Vicente's brown nipple. It had an unexpectedly pleasant effect.

"If you keep doing that, you will be filled with my cum soon."

Hans was a mischievous man. He reached up with both hands and twisted the nipples. He licked them, sucked them, and plucked them before returning to pinching them from afar. He lay back and closed his eyes. "Such pleasure is more than any man can bear." He gave another tug on the nipples until Vicente's precum leaked from the tip of the monster.

Whatever hormones were in that clear liquid immediately affected Hans, who thrashed about in ecstasy.

"Da. Da. Da." The blue-eyed boy was glimpsing heaven, or so Vicente believed based on the faraway gaze.

Hans pinched hard on Vicente's nipples, triggering a chain reaction that could not be undone. The Mexican felt ripples from his belly through his balls and down the length of his cock. They grew more intense as his balls churned. He pounded so hard, he thought he might kill the poor priest, but Hans pinched twice as hard: Vicente exploded. The whole lower digestive tract was coated in olive oil and cum, and ever more semen was pumping into the young man. Soon it exploded around the sides of Vicente's cock, out of the anus and onto the carpet and couch. Hans erupted a second time, adding to the mess. Vicente, worried that a servant could enter at any moment, hastily removed his entire cock from Hans. This sent Hans into a paroxysm of convulsions that looked bad until Vicente saw the smile.

"Oh yes! Oh yes! Ohhhhhh!" He jerked his little cock until it gave its third release. He looked up at Vicente and grinned. "You give me orgasm like a woman."

7

PAYING THE PIPER

That night at the orgy, Vicente was brought before the oracle. "You spilled your seed in an outsider."

"Yes, I did. Hans is my friend."

"That is a sin against me. Your semen is for my acolytes only."

"I can't undo it."

"No, but I can punish you. I will enlist Hans in our festivities for eternity starting tomorrow."

Vicente was wracked with guilt. He clearly had no privacy. There were probably peepholes in the wall and microphones taped to the underside of the furniture. "Why do you spy on me?"

"Asmodeus sees all, knows all. You cannot break free."

The following day, Vicente thought about the mysteries he read as a child. They were written by an American and translated into hundreds of languages. Mysterios de los Hardy Boys. They were very well written. And there was a common theme in many of the books. A ghost or some other supernatural being was intended to frighten people away. The Hardy Boys never gave up. They unmasked the human playing a ghost or the devil and sent them packing. He returned to his earlier theory that he was being spied upon, and information was then fed to the oracle. He pulled out the sigil for Asmodeus from his desk drawer as a plan came to mind.

At Vespers, Vicente shifted nervously in his seat. The prayers were all comforting to him because they were the saints' familiar, divinely inspired words. The darkness in the pit of the church gave him great bodily pleasure but stole away his spirit. He hoped that would all change tonight. He enjoyed sex but not sexual slavery. He was a stallion but not a stud. His semen was not an elixir to make the young priests powerful. It was just damn good semen. And it was his. He may have given his life to the church, but not his manhood.

There had been so much anal sex in the temple; it smelled like sweat, ass, fire, and brimstone. It was the smell of hell itself.

The oracle sat in a trance. He beckoned Vicente over.

"Tonight, you will fill every vessel. I need your seed to plant the crops of pleasure."

Vicente surreptitiously let the sigil drop from under his robe. The oracle continued.

"You are a slave, but someday you shall rule at my right hand."

"Did you drop this?"

Vicente picked up the sigil and handed it to the oracle. The withered old man frowned. "What is this? It's just rubbish."

"You don't recognize it?" Vicente was at the edge of a precipice.

The oracle frowned again. "No. This is not mine. Burn it."

If Asmodeus were genuinely inhabiting the oracle's body, he should have recognized the sigil and would then have to grant Vicente a wish. They were frauds! This made his remaining plans much more straightforward. He would play along tonight, but his plan was unfolding.

Out of the corner of his eye, he saw a lock of blond hair fighting off his oppressors. "Let go of me! You devil worshippers!"

Hans had pluck and daring. This group would surely beat it out of him if he kept it up. I made a point of moving into a position where I would be with him first. He saw me and looked away angrily.

"Hey, hey, Hans. What's wrong?"

"They told me you recruited me. That fuck was an audition for your patron demon."

"Lies. More than you know."

"Yes, I saw through them. It is not with you that I'm angry."

"Silence!" Cardinale Beluomo shocked the room into submission. "Let the Carnevale begin."

Cardinals lined up before their novitiates, prepared for their nightly orgy. Drinks were passed around. Hans became giddy; Vicente sported an erection hard as diamonds.

He whispered to his friend. "I was rough on you yesterday; will you be okay?"

Hans smiled and patted his nether region, which had swollen and stretched. "I cannot hear my farts today. I am still stretched." To illustrate his point, Hans pushed open his hole, revealing a rosy red interior.

"Isn't it sore?"

"No. Do it. All at once."

Vicente's cock glistened with lard. He pointed it at the loose hole of his friend and entered with no resistance. The combination of the mead and his earlier fucking had turned Hans from a door to a hallway. Vicente easily popped past the anus, slid down the chute, rounded the bend, and struck home. Hans jerked violently, but his face betrayed the pleasure the massive cock gave him. "Hans, we must speak."

Vicente lifted the light priest, who wrapped his legs around his partner's waist. "I know a place."

Vicente took the boy to the dark corner where Cardinal Highsmith, the Australian, had taken him that first night.

Hans lay his head on Vicente's strong shoulder. "I'm listening."

Vicente recounted his tale of the sigil and the proof that Asmodeus was a fiction. Hans just groaned with pleasure as he rode the pole like a pony. Vicente set the blond down on the dirt floor.

"I want you inside me all the time, Padre." Vicente blushed in the dark. He wasn't a Padre yet, just studying to become one, or so he thought before his imprisonment.

Vicente said, "We must get out of this trap first."

Hans reached up and planted a wet kiss on the lips. "Take me with you."

Vicente felt a stirring in his chest. For the first time, he felt his heart skip a beat. He wanted Hans badly and forever.

"I would never leave you, my darling." Vicente was embarrassed by his words.

Hans kissed him feverishly. "Do it, fuck my brains out."

Vicente gave a repeat performance of yesterday's bludgeoning. The darkness made it all the more magical, as did the love he felt for his friend. He pounded hard, leaving Hans in a stupor. The little blond man twisted and jerked beneath the swarthy Mexican. He moaned with pleasure each time Vicente hit that spot deep inside him where the passageway turned yet again. When the head of the massive cock traveled back through the colorectal valve, both men uttered a sigh. Vicente because the sensation of pulling his cockhead through such a tight turn left him reeling with pleasure. When he thrust his way back through with a loud pop, they both sucked air between their teeth. Hans did it because he was sensitive to the pain bordering on pleasure, and Vicente because he worried he was hurting his friend. But Hans made sounds that proved he loved every inch of Vicente inside him.

In near-complete darkness, the two men had to feel their way to orgasm. Vicente grabbed Hans by the cock and jerked him. Hans pushed him away. "No, I am too close!" But it was too late. Vicente felt wet spurts of Swiss cum on his wrist, hand, chest, and face.

The smell alone was enough to push Vicente over the edge. With a final thrust that caused Hans to shriek, Vicente emptied his balls in giant spurts. He remained inside Hans for a while, kissing him and stroking his hair. He stayed too long; his cock fired back up and stretched Hans like a balloon.

"Are you good for another?"

"Ja."

Vicente caressed Hans lovingly, picked him up, and whispered, "I will find a way to get us out of this mess." But Hans was far away on top of pleasure mountain, the highest peak in Italy. Vicente thrust instinctively, then with purpose. He wanted to hit that spot that made Hans moan. Instead of long, hard strokes, he stayed buried deeply and continued hitting that spot. The moans turned into howls of pleasure. Bam! Bam! Bam! He kept hitting that spot where the sigmoid colon turns North. Hans began to spasm violently. Vicente sailed away on a ship of bliss. He sensed only Hans and nothing else.

"Are you okay? Have I hurt you?"

"No," Hans said. "I'm coming deep in my belly."

The spasms ended. "You made me cum like a woman."

Vicente's arms grew tired. His mind returned to the dimly lit orgy. He continued thrusting, pushing the magic button. When Hans lay on the leather hammock, he put his knees beside his ears. In the light, Vicente could see the gaping hole he had created in his friend. It turned him on so much that he felt another orgasm coming. Hans must have sensed it because he took his small Swiss prick in his fingers and pumped hard. In perfect sync, the two men ejaculated a second time. They remained silent, locked, and vibrant. The cramps running up and down Hans's insides milked the last of the sperm from Vicente's giant cock. When The monster finally grew soft, those same cramps pushed the massive slab of meat out of the colon and then out of the rectum. The boy's anus remained wide open like a cave for a moment, fully exposing the bright red rectum. Then it snapped shut and returned to looking like a little tight pink hole again. Vicente watched, fascinated, as the man's anus opened again, revealing the grey lips inside the sphincter; they had formed due to all the friction. The third time the rectum opened, a river of cum ran from the man's ass, puddling on the floor.

Vicente smiled as he heard Hans laugh at the other men who entered him. He was so stretched out; probably even the biggest of the Cardinals just felt like a feather tickling him. Vicente did his nightly duty, stretching open the novitiates who were ready and bringing them to orgasm. Hans shot jealous glances, but Vicente was obliged to fuck everyone that could handle him. Without that warm feeling in his chest, the sex was empty. He tried to focus on pleasing his partners, but his mind revisited the incredible sex with his friend Hans. After what felt like an eternity, the ceremony ended. Every cardinal was spent, and a few were also gaping from the fucking Vicente had given them. Everyone whom Vicente had fucked was limping. Hans, too, was walking awkwardly up the stone staircase. Vicente pushed ahead and lifted Hans onto his shoulders.

The short man had to duck through doorways. They

laughed with the joy of two young children playing in a meadow of flowers. This was not well received by the Cardinals.

Early the following day, Hans knocked on Vicente's door. He stepped inside with a scowl.

"What is it, mi cariño?"

Hans shook his head. "Cardinale Beluomo forbids us from having sex again. He said we had too much fun and lost focus on giving pleasure to Asmodeus."

The thought of having to fuck all those men and not Hans caused Vicente to weep.

Hans punched his arm. "Hey, friend, we will find a way, da?"

Very quietly, they sat on the cum-stained sofa and plotted. Hans said he would find all the peepholes and microphones under the guise of helping Vicente clean the apartment. Vicente agreed to travel the hallway in search of exits.

The big Mexican strode down the hall, seeking exit points. A Swiss Guard appeared.

"May I help you, sir?"

"I'm looking for the way to the Basilica. I wish to pray there."

"No, I'm sorry. All who live on this floor are forbidden from leaving unattended." Vicente watched the man's eyes as they darted to a door and back. The door had no room number and was shaped like an archway.

Vicente walked to the door and tested the knob. "May I use the bathroom?"

"That's a staircase, not a bathroom!"

He opened the door. "Oh, so it is. Sorry for troubling you."

The Swiss Guard glared at him. To distract him, Vicente shifted his soft cock under his robes. It was a magic talisman. The guard's eyes widened, and his attention drifted from Vicente to the massive cock outlined by the robes.

"Uh, it's no trouble, man. No trouble at all."

He stared, mesmerized by the monster that hid under Vicente's clothes. The priest dropped his room key. When he bent over to retrieve it, he hiked his skirts high so the end of his dick was exposed to open air.

When he stood, the Swiss Guard wiped sweat from his brow.

"What's your name, young man?" Vicente was maybe two years older but wanted to establish his dominance over the lad.

"Gaetano, sir."

"Gaetano, such a fine name for a handsome young man."

The guard couldn't stop staring at the extraordinary bulge under Vicente's frock. Stammering, he said, "I can show you where the restroom is."

Vicente was gathering intelligence, and this tidbit of knowledge might be helpful.

"Okay, Gaetano, take me to the restroom."

They passed Vicente's room. "That's mine. We could go there."

The Guard shook his head. "Not a good idea."

This confirmed his suspicions that he had no privacy in his room.

The hallway continued for a long time. Gaetano was sporting a stiff one in his clown knickers. Vicente looked back and smiled. "I sure appreciate you doing this. How can I pay you back?"

Gaetano smiled. He said softly, "I'll tell you when we arrive. This hallway is monitored." More intelligence.

At long last, they reached the men's room. There were two doors, and both of them were very squeaky. The guard held the first door for Vicente and followed him in.

In the fever of youth, Gaetano mauled Vicente's lips

with his. He tore at his clothing, unbuttoning the frilly collar, discarding his jacket, and pulling down his knickers. The keys attached to his pants hit the ground with a loud clatter.

Gaetano pulled Vicente's linen robe over his head. The priest was naked. Vicente recalled how often he had been naked and concluded that he spent more time out of his clothes than in them. The young guard grabbed Vicente's ass and cradled the round cheeks in his big hands.

The surprise came when Gaetano shucked his underpants. He was sporting a long, thick hardon, far larger than Vicente anticipated.

"Bend over." The guard took over. He fit his thick pole into the priest with spit and manual stretching. It had been a while since a cock had visited his hole, but Vicente felt no discomfort when Gaetano pushed his way inside. "Yeah. Take it. You know you want it." He repeated himself like a parrot.

Vicente had to admit, a good fuck in the ass was something he wanted.

Gaetano was one of those men who treated other men like wild game to be bagged. To fuck someone as hung as Vicente was probably a white rhino for the lad. The guard reached around and stroked Vicente, who was still growing hard. He was happy to give his ass to this young man. Hans would not be as happy about it, but it was for a good cause. Vicente needed to string this one along until the moment they needed to make a dash for it. His keys would no doubt get them out of their jail.

Gaetano would one day become one of those men with thick cocks who take hours to cum. At this age, he was ready in minutes.

"Oh shit! Fu-u-u-u-ck." Gaetano was at the precipice. He fired his warm load into Vicente's ass. He rubbed the priest's back. "Mmm, your skin is so brown and soft."

Vicente remained silent. He was eyeballing the key chain, planning their eventual use in the escape.

"Hey man, aren't you gonna cum?"

Vicente realized he hadn't done his part. "I can only cum with your dick in my mouth."

Gaetano needed no convincing. He pushed the priest to his knees. He took a wide masculine stance.

Vicente felt guilty over how much he enjoyed sucking Gaetano's choke-thick cock. He wasn't very experienced in fellatio, so he coughed and spat up a few times before finally getting used to the massive meat stick down his throat.

"Yeah, I make you gag, don't I, little bitch." He slapped Vicente softly, then harder. "Answer me!"

"Mnh, Mm-hm." Vicente could scarcely get air to leave his lungs. Gaetano dragged Vicente into a toilet stall and made him lie down with his legs and cock against the wall and his back draped over the toilet seat. As Vicente leaned his head back, Gaetano plunged the entire length and girth of his cock down Vicente's throat and held it there. Vicente coughed, gagged, and rivulets of thick saliva cascaded out of his mouth and onto his nose, eyes, and hair. Gaetano used him like a hand, masturbating himself with his lips and throat. He held his head and pulled him by the ears.

"That's why we call fags big ears. Faggot." It was an act. Vicente wasn't worried. He did need to perform for the lad, so he stroked his enormous cock vigorously until it was standing straight up in the air. He couldn't reach the end from this angle, so he concentrated on wrapping both his hands around the base and stroking the bottom portion. Gaetano took pity on him. He leaned forward and licked the piss slit.

"Mmm. Mexican food."

Vicente would have laughed if he weren't gagged on

Gaetano's thick little monster. Gaetano's tongue grew more forceful, stretching the pee hole until he could curl up his tongue like a taco and jam it down there. Vicente liked it, but he needed more. He reached up helplessly until the guard took the hint. He massaged the head and shaft while he fucked Vicente's face.

Vicente continued to cough and splutter, soaking his face in frothy spit. Gaetano pulled out just in time for Vicente to avoid passing out, then plunged it deep, past the tonsils and into the esophagus.

Vicente knew he had to hurry. Gaetano's cock tasted like sweet precum. It was only a matter of moments. He thought about Hans. He imagined himself fucking the little Swiss man. It helped. When Gaetano bypassed Vicente's throat and shot ropes of cum down his gullet, it was enough to put him over. Vicente's cock grew even more massive before it exploded with cum. It rained down on both men.

"I gotta get back to work." He smacked Vicente's ass. "Let's do this again."

Vicente was obliged to pretend that he was looking forward to it. "Yeah, man. What are good days for you?"

"I don't work Tuesdays. Any other day, just drop by, and we can fuck and suck for an hour or more."

Vicente would have lost track of the calendar if it weren't for the massive crowds in St. Peter's Square every Sunday. He knew today was Wednesday. He had five more days to lure Gaetano away from his post and boost the keys.

The guard was still buttoning up his coat as he ran out of the restroom. Vicente looked at his reflection. He was covered in a mucus and saliva stew. His black hair was practically white. He washed up as best he could and hurried back to his room.

8

HATCHING A PLAN

Hans greeted him with a kiss and pulled away. "Oh, are you sick? I taste vomit."

Vicente nodded. It was a lie, but it was silent.

"You should lie down."

"No, no, it was just something I ate. I'm better now." His voice croaked like a frog.

"Nonsense. I'll make you a tea with lemon and honey. Hmm?"

Vicente's throat was raw. The tea sounded good.

Hans went to his room and returned with a steaming mug of chamomile. The herbs, honey, and lemon all soothed Vicente's throat.

The priest looked at the blond cherub and said, "Did you find anything?"

Hans held his finger to his lips. He motioned for Vicente to follow him into the bathroom.

"Okay, there's a bug in your living room. I don't know how to deactivate it without arousing suspicion."

Vicente smiled, "That's good. We can use it to feed them false information."

"I also found three peepholes—one in here, one in the living room, and one in your bedroom. There are a few blind spots in the house, so I will mark them for you. Also, I put a glass vase in front of the bedroom and living room holes. It will distort the view but make it appear innocent. Fill it with flowers from the orgy room."

"So, no bugs in the bathroom?"

"I imagine they draw the line somewhere." Hans giggled. "What did you find out?"

Vicente paused to put it delicately. "I found a door to a stair. It's unlocked, but I am sure it leads to a locked door."

"It's a start."

"But there's more. I met Gaetano, a Swiss Guard. He has a ring of keys on his belt loop."

Hans shrugged. "Sounds difficult."

"No, um, he likes to look at me down there. He gets very distracted."

"You hypnotize him with your cock?" They both laughed.

Vicente said, "I'm certain I can get those keys from him, but it will have to be on the day we escape. He'll know within minutes that they're gone." He felt guilty for not coming clean about his sexual escapades. It wasn't too late to tell the truth.

"I have to blow him, though."

Hans shrugged. "We do what we must." He wasn't as bothered as Vicente expected. Or perhaps he was hiding it well.

"Are you okay with that, Hans? Really?"

"I was okay from the moment you walked in with dick on your breath and spittle in your hair. Truly. We do what we must to survive."

The bathroom was very cramped, but Vicente managed to position Hans so he could penetrate him. He put his hand on the ledge, covering the peephole. The sight of Hans' loose hole made Vicente very hard. His cock swelled up quickly, filling the bathroom with its mass. He had to back into the bedroom just to be able to position himself for penetration. Hans welcomed the throbbing log of flesh into his hole. He gave no resistance. Vicente could glide easily on the remnants of lard from the previous night. This time, he had no problem reaching climax. In fact, he struggled not to cum until Hans had done so. Hans didn't need his hands to come. Vicente tapping on that button deep inside was all the stimulation he needed.

"Oh, da! Da! Da!" Hans shot cum into the toilet.

Vicente was right behind him. "Si! Si! Si!" He unloaded a torrent of sperm into his friend, who was quickly becoming a lover.

They showered together and prepared for Vespers and the debauchery that came after.

Now that Hans and Vicente knew what they could and couldn't do in the various rooms of the apartment, sex became a staple for them. Every morning Hans arrived well before breakfast and shuffled into the bathroom, presenting his gaping hole for Vicente, who never tired of filling it with his semen.

Breakfast usually arrived at eight o'clock. There was enough for five people, so Hans always stayed and ate heartily. His apartment had a little kitchen, and he was expected to prepare his own meals from the groceries they brought him.

If it weren't for the sexual slavery, Vicente could have grown comfortable. He had three magnificent meals a day, a sex partner who could easily accommodate his massive prick, and all the luxuries the Vatican could provide. But he and Hans were prisoners with velvet handcuffs. And when the cuffs came off, it was for a stinky, loud, abhorrent orgy of priests and Cardinals built on lies and deceit.

Later that week, Vicente lured Gaetano back into the bathroom. He wanted a closer look at the snap that held the keys. He got quite a bit more than that. The guard fucked him brutally, drawing blood, and pounded his throat. When Vicente limped into Vespers with a hoarse 'Hello,' Hans smiled and said, "We do what we must to survive."

They hadn't set a date for their escape, so circumstances set the date for them. Pope Pius VI died. The entire College of Cardinals was in a panic. Who should succeed him? Who will make the funeral arrangements? Of course, the Vatican had endured dozens of dead Popes, perhaps hundreds, so there was a drill. Hans and Vicente agreed that they must strike while the iron was hot.

The first wrinkle in the plan came when Vicente realized it was Tuesday and Gaetano was off duty. A much older, more muscular man stood guard.

"What are you doing here? You should be in your room!"

Vicente thought fast. "Is that the restroom?" He pointed to the arched doorway.

"None of your damned business. Get back into your room."

Undaunted, Vicente adjusted his cock visibly. The guard pretended not to notice. Bult Vicente positioned it so it protruded. The Guard's eyes darted downward.

Vicente kept at it. "I really don't need to go to the bathroom. I just want to."

He shifted, and his pendulous cock fell from his hip; the Swiss Guard cleared his throat. His gaze was fixed now. He licked his lips.

"I'm Vicente." He extended his hand.

"Giorgio."

"Giorgio, would you like to escort me to the restroom?"

The silence was deafening.

Vicente turned with a tilt of the head and began walking down the hallway toward the restroom. He broke into a grin when he heard heavy footfalls behind him.

❧ 9 ❧
THE WAY OUT

Vicente had misjudged the situation. Once they were in the privacy of the restroom, Giorgio punched him in the face.

"Faggot!"

Vicente's nose ran with blood. He came to his senses before the guard could land another blow. Vicente charged him like a luchador. Giorgio was a stocky man, but Vicente's height gave him leverage. He rammed his shoulder into Giorgio's chest, sending him sprawling. Before Giorgio could get up, Vicente punched him. Then he punched him again. Giorgio had a strong constitution. He struggled to get up. Vicente leaned into the man, his palm flat on his chest.

"Giorgio, I'm going to help you to your feet if you promise not to try anything like that again. But I'll beat you senseless if you can't make that promise."

Giorgio nodded.

Vicente put one hand on Giorgio's hip and gripped his hand, hauling him upright. The Swiss Guard looked dazed. At the hip, Vicente unsnapped the keys, pocketing them silently.

Giorgio snarled. "I need to take a piss, so get the fuck out."

Vicente scurried back to his apartment, where Hans was waiting anxiously.

"Did you get them?"

Vicente stepped into one of the blind spots and dangled the keys. "We really have to leave this instant, though. The guard I took them from beat me, and he was pretty rough."

Hans dabbed at the bruise under Vicente's eye. "Now. We go now."

The two priests walked calmly down the hallway to the arched doorway.

"Hey! You!" Giorgio ran down the hallway toward them.

The two yanked open the door in a flash and ran down the stairs. Just as Vicente imagined, there was a locked door.

Hans fumbled with the keys; the first one didn't turn, then he dropped the keyring. The door above opened. "You faggot sons of bitches!"

Hans retrieved the keys, trying another. It didn't work. Then he tried a third, and the lock clicked open. He pushed Vicente through the door, but Giorgio was on them. The brute grabbed Hans by the neck. "Go without me, Vicente."

"Never!" Vicente unleashed his rage on Giorgio, pounding his face until his knuckles were bloody. Giorgio struggled to get the keys, but Hans put them in Vicente's pocket, out of sight. Hans' face changed from red to blue. He would suffocate soon. Vicente landed a blow that sent Giorgio staggering. He released Hans as he struggled to regain his foothold. The portly guard collapsed to the floor, out cold.

Come on! Vicente grabbed Hans and pulled him through, slamming the door behind them. He tested it; it was locked.

Hans couldn't catch his breath. He took long, deep

inhales until the blue drained from his face. Vicente smiled. "We did it!"

Hans managed to squeak out a reply. "Not yet. Not by a longshot."

They looked around. It looked remarkably like the floor above, meaning a Swiss Guard was probably roaming the halls. They found the arched door, but just as they were about to open it, the Guard came around a corner.

"Hey! What do you two think you are doing?"

Vicente had thought this through in advance. "I'm sorry, sir, we're Jesuits visiting from our seminary in Mexico. We seem to have gotten lost."

Hans nodded to confirm.

The Guard didn't know them or where they belonged. He was friendly. "It happens all the time. This place is like a maze. Where were you trying to go?"

Hans had no voice, so Vicente continued the charade. "Well, I heard that Michelangelo's Pieta' is one of the world's most beautiful sculptures, but I didn't see it in St. Peter's, so we wandered off, and here we are."

The Guard laughed. "It's right on the main floor of the Basilica, silly. You didn't see it?"

"No, and we don't know our way back."

The guard hooked elbows with them and escorted them into a vestibule. He pushed a button.

"What's this?" Vicente asked.

In answer, a tiny bell sounded, and the wall opened up along an invisible seam—a tiny elevator.

"I need to use my keys to get you out of this restricted area. Hang on." He fumbled with the keys and pressed the G button. "It's a bit slow, but it will get you there."

A loud pounding and bellowing startled the guard. It was coming from behind the locked door they had just come through.

The guard smiled. "My comrade Giorgio is a drunk.

That's why he only works relief shifts. I'd better let you go."

He pinched Hans on the ass before he left them. The elevator doors closed, and they ascended. The doors opened in a vestibule behind the altar. The church was crawling with tourists. Many were kneeling in prayer, tearful over the loss of Pius XII.

Hans took Vicente by the hand and pulled him deeper into the crowd. "Strength in numbers."

Ensuring they were in the thickest part of the throng, they slowly approached the exit. At the exit, there was a sign with two arrows. One arrow read "Piazza San Pietro," and the other "Controllo di Passaporto."

Hans whispered in Vicente's ear. "The Piazza is part of the Vatican but on Italian soil.

Vicente had been imprisoned almost from the moment he arrived. He couldn't navigate because he had never even been in St. Peter's, only below it in the bowels. Hans, however, was an expert guide. He had been at the Vatican for several months before the Asmodeans imprisoned him.

For a brief instant, Vicente wondered if Asmodeus would smite him. He shook his head, answering his own question. The whole experience had changed his faith in God and the Catholic Church.

Dazzled by the Italian sun, Vicente and Hans wandered across the tiles and stones that lay in intricate patterns on the Piazza San Pietro.

Vicente and Hans were penniless but dressed in their priest's garb.

"It will be easier to go to my seminary in Switzerland than yours in Mexico." Hans was a practical thinker.

"I agree. Besides, my superior who sent me here knew exactly what would become of me. I never want to see that bastard again."

Hans nodded. He had not been sent into sexual slavery like Vicente.

"I think we must not tell of what befell us there. It is better to say we were thrown out for having sex with one another."

Vicente agreed. "Yes. But I will find a way to end that cabal of warlocks."

Hans smiled. "You might not have to. They're electing a new Pope. The fate of every Cardinal rests on the conclave."

At an antique dealer, Vicente sold the keys to the secret chambers for 28,000 Lire, which was about fifty US Dollars or 1200 Mexican Pesos—enough for two train tickets to Switzerland and a couple of meals.

Hans took Vicente to Giolitti, the gelateria, where he procured two rich chocolate cones with whipped cream below and above the scoop. Vicente had never seen ruins. He stopped at every little corner where a piece of Ancient Rome had crumbled and fallen into the modern world. There were places where an ancient Roman wall ran headlong into a minimalist modern apartment building. Vicente's enthusiasm had a positive effect on Hans. He knew much about Rome and shared his knowledge at every opportunity.

BENEDICTINE BLISS

The train for Zurich leaves every hour. The ride is 9 hours long. After dining at a hole in the wall with incredible food, the duo hopped on the night train. They had enough to book a private room, so they did.

In the room, Vicente removed his robe, allowing his member to sway from side to side with the train's motion. Hans put lotion on the massive cock, then deftly inserted the head into his ass. Vicente grew hard, pressing his way into his lover. It took the entire bottle of lotion, but Vicente wormed his way past the junction to the spot that made Hans cum with no hands.

The rocking of the train made small work for Vicente. He was naturally tapping on the button without any voluntary motion. The vibration of the train added even more pleasure.

"Yes, meinen Liebhaber." Hans growled and moaned. He jerked involuntarily every time the tip of Vicente's cock pressed that spot on his descending colon. The jerking made Vicente increasingly aroused, which caused his cock to swell further, which increased the frequency with which he tapped the spot. It was a virtuous circle of pleasure.

Hans shot a load into the sink. Seeing it put Vicente

over the edge, and he released his sperm inside the little man.

Still deep inside Hans, Vicente dragged him to the tiny bed, where they spooned until Vicente got hard again. They made a game of not moving, letting the train do the fucking. Vicente stayed inside Hans the entire night. He came inside him more times than he could count. He even woke up to an orgasm. Hans soiled the linen with his cum. It pooled and puddled throughout the night until they arrived in Zurich.

"My abbey is a short train ride from here. Come." Hans held out his hand, and Vicente took it.

The train ride was breathtaking. As the train skirted Lake Zurich, Vicente marveled at the snow-capped peaks of Mount Titlis rising out of the dark green foothills.

Abbot Rosserute looked puzzled when he saw the two priests approaching the monastery.

"Allo, Abt Rosserute!" Hans gave the man a warm hug.

For Vicente's benefit, they spoke in the lingua franca - which had become English since the wars.

"Hans, why are you here?"

Hans smiled. "It was time to come home."

"Who ist your friend? A priest, ja?"

Vicente stepped forward and offered his hand. "Vicente Pesante, from Mexico."

Abbot Rosserute took the big brown hand into his and shook. "I still do not understand what would cause you to leave Vatican City. Is this a holiday?"

Hans found it easiest to explain the situation in German. Vicente knew enough to tell that no lies were being concocted, only the ugly truth. As Hans continued, the Abbot's face turned grey, then white. When Hans finished, the Abbot punched his fist into his palm.

"Pius XII embodied all that's wrong with the Church."

Hans nodded. "Ja. And now he's dead. Have they elected a new Pope yet?"

Abbot Rosserute nodded. "Yes. A Cardinal Beluomo is rising to the new position. I don't know that he's picked a name yet."

Hans and Vicente shared a glance. Vicente added, "He is in the Asmodean council. A worshipper of Asmodeus. Perhaps the worst." Vicente recalled the brutal fucking he got from Cardinal Beluomo on his first day. He was the man who decided to lock Vicente in chambers.

Abbot Rosserute nodded. "I have met the man. There was something wrong with him."

Hans said, "He had a cock like two soup cans stacked on each other."

Vicente gasped, scandalized by the rude language.

The Abbot laughed heartily. "Thicker than mine?"

Hans nodded but added quickly, "But not as long."

Vicente was drawn to the man's robes, seeking an indication of his size. The Abbot playfully rocked his hips, revealing a terribly long penis beneath the cloth.

Hans pointed to Vicente. "His is longer and thicker."

Abbot Rosserute smiled. "We are not hypocrites, Vicente. We are open about sex between monks. You have nothing to fear. And we hold no prisoners."

That night, after supper, Vicente learned what it felt like to be fucked by a horse-hung man. It was peculiar to feel the cock snake around in his colon. There was not much pain; the Abbot's cock was thick but not excessively so. While Vicente took the pounding of his life, he slipped inside Hans, filling him completely. The Abbot set the pace. He thrust at a rapid clip, which caused Vicente to tap the innermost part of Hans in quick succession. Hans, with his little penis, was able to ejaculate multiple times. Vicente had filled Hans with his cum to the point that it sprayed out with each thrust.

The two young men were outpaced by this marathon fucker with a horse cock. They were at the point where each new orgasm was too much. When the older man finally reached orgasm, the two younger priests breathed relief. Vicente marveled at the spreading warmth deep in his belly. He was still hard inside Hans, who wriggled with delight. The Abbot, too, was still rock hard. Eventually, their tumescence subsided. In synchronous peristaltic waves, Hans pushed out Vicente while Vicente pushed out Abbot Rosserute. The two monsters were expelled simultaneously, so they landed on the floor with a loud "thunk!" followed by a waterfall of priest semen. The three men stayed close all night in the Abbot's big bed. In the morning, Vicente decided he had found his home. He and Hans shared a room where they would live freely together until the end of their days.

ABOUT PETER SCHUTES

Peter Schutes is a fictional character. He was modeled after the gay pulp fiction authors of the 1970s and 1980s. His creator often wondered who the men were who wrote these books, and so he created Peter to satisfy his curiosity.

Peter was born in 1896 to a wealthy New England family. His whole life, he carried a massive burden: he had a gigantic penis. His sex life was defined by the men who worshipped him.

Peter led a tempestuous life, which is documented in the fictional masterpiece "The Autobiography of Peter Schutes." To learn more about this prolific and prodigious author, we recommend reading his immortal tale of life with too much of a good thing.

ABOUT ADAM MAXWELL BIGGLESWORTH

Adam Maxwell Bigglesworth was a fictional protegé of prolific and prodigious author Peter Schutes. His fiction contains similar themes. We at Peter Schutes Publishing found several well-polished manuscripts by this author among Peter's possessions. We know little about the author except for one letter we found. Adam was raised in England but emigrated to Santa Monica, California, in the late 1970s. He had a brief affair with Peter, but he wasn't flexible enough to handle the legendary beast, so they became friends and colleagues.

Look for more short stories and novellas by this new, imaginary voice under the Peter Schutes Publishing imprint.

OTHER BOOKS FROM PETER SCHUTES PUBLISHING

E-books and Paperbacks (as noted)

The Able Seaman

The Anaconda Copper

The Autobiography of Peter Schutes*

Backwoods Delivery

Big Bodies of All Sizes*

Big Hole River*

Bobbing Buoys and Salty Seamen*

Bunkhouse Buddies*

The Butt Baby*

Cloistered

Confessions of a Rodeo Clown*

Dark as a Dungeon*

Demonic Deception *aka* Deceived, Cursed & Blessed

Desert Island Daddies

The Expectant Member

Firehouse Lovers

The Fish

Five Erotic Tales*

The Gospel of Priapus*

Hercules and Lippos

Hobo Honey

Hot Blue Collars*

Hotshot

Logger's Delight

Muscle Bottom*

Panama Heat

Satan's Sissy Boy

The Slaves of Rome*

The Thigh Baby

Under the Boardwalk

World's Biggest

Coming Soon

Backwoods Delivery - The Complete Daddy's Boy Series

Like the Greeks Do*

Higher Education*

Hoboes, Hustlers, and Jailbirds*

Small Cockpits and Big Hangars*

Tales of Two Daddies*

*Available as Paperbacks

www.ingramcontent.com/pod-product-compliance
Lightning Source LLC
Chambersburg PA
CBHW011143310726
48972CB00009B/2831